The BEASTS of KNOBBLY BOTTOM

ATTACK OF THE VAMPIRE SHEEP

EMILY-JANE CLARK

SCHOLASTIC

Published in the UK by Scholastic, 2023
1 London Bridge, London, SE1 9BG
Scholastic Ireland, 89E Lagan Road, Dublin Industrial Estate,
Glasnevin, Dublin, D11 HP5F

Text © Emily-Jane Clark, 2023
Illustrations by Jeff Crowther © Scholastic, 2023

ISBN 978 0702 32510 6

A CIP catalogue record for this book is available from the British
Library.

Printed and bound in Great Britain by Clays Ltd, Elcograf S.p.A
Paper made from wood grown in sustainable forests and other
controlled sources.

MIX
Paper | Supporting
responsible forestry
FSC® C018072

1 3 5 7 9 10 8 6 4 2

www.scholastic.co.uk

For Isla and Cleo

CONTENTS

CHAPTER ONE

Secrets and (my mum's) big fat lies

My name is Maggie McKay and I have a BIG secret.

It all started when my mum decided to RUIN MY LIFE by making us move from our perfectly nice flat in Leicester to a stupid house in **Knobbly Bottom**.

I suppose I should tell you that **Knobbly Bottom** is *not* an actual bottom with knobbly bits on it. It is a small village in England. Although I wished it *was* an actual bottom, so I could give

it a flipping big kick all the way to Australia. Then we *definitely* wouldn't have had to move, as my mum said she would *never* go to Australia because of the ginormous spiders.

As you may have guessed, my BIG secret is in **Knobbly Bottom** – THE VILLAGE, NOT THE BUM.

But I should start by telling you a bit about me.

I am nine years old and although this is a LARGE number, I am the smallest person in my class.

Mum says being small is actually a **superpower** because I can fit into really tiny spaces and so I always win at hide-and-seek.

My nana keeps saying I might be like Uncle Mick,

who used to be really small but then "shot up" to six feet when he turned twelve! I'm not sure I fancy shooting up to six feet when I turn twelve. It sounds blimming painful if you ask me.

I might be the smallest person in my class, but I am *not* the smallest person in my family, because I have a little sister called Lily.

Lily is obsessed with superheroes and ice cream, and everyone thinks she's cute. But you should know that she uses her cuteness for evil.

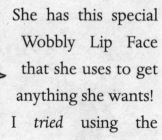 She has this special Wobbly Lip Face that she uses to get anything she wants! I *tried* using the Wobbly Lip Face to get another biscuit the other day, but Mum just asked if there was something wrong with my mouth! So I said, "Yes, actually, my mouth wants a biscuit." But she told me to tell my mouth that it would have to wait until after dinner.

Which brings me to the fact that I also have one grown-up called Lucy, who is my mum. She calls us the **Fantastic Three** and says that there is *nothing* we can't do together. Although this isn't technically true, because once we tried to build a cabin bed from IKEA and we definitely could NOT do that.

I like strawberry milkshakes, gel pens and biscuits, and I am good at throwing stuff. Balls mainly, but sometimes other things. Sticks, loo roll tubes into the bathroom bin, and once I chucked a conker all the way to Mars! Mum also says that I am really good at making up stories.

So that's me! Maggie McKay – a short but VERY BRAVE champion thing-thrower, biscuit-lover and **HERO** of this book.

Now as you may have guessed, I completely, utterly-with-knobs-on did *not* want to move to a boring little village, so I tried *everything* to stop us from leaving Leicester.

When I say *everything*, I mostly just shouted "I'M NOT GOING TO Knobbly Bottom" over and over again, and stamped my feet a lot, which is how Lily has got her way loads of times.

"Fine, Maggie," my mum said. "But me and Lily are going so you'll have to stay here all on your own!"

Then she went ON and ON about how the

countryside is a "much safer place to bring up children", and I told her I don't have any children so I don't really care about that.

"And I know for a FACT that the countryside is NOT safe at all because Violet Parker from my class went there for a weekend and broke her leg in TWO places," I added.

"She fell out of a tree, Maggie," my mum said. "It's hardly the countryside's fault."

"It *is* the countryside's fault for being a *wilderness* full of evil danger trees," I said. "I climb trees in Leicester all the time and I've never even broken my leg in *one* place!"

"Well, maybe you are just better at climbing trees than Violet," my mum said, and I couldn't really argue with that because I *am* better at climbing trees than Violet.

Then Mum said that the BEST thing about

the countryside is that the air is much cleaner than it is in the city, which is also NOT true. If you have ever been *unlucky* enough to get a whiff of **Knobbly Bottom**, you'll know it smells like cow poo. This is because of a thing called *muck spreading*. I KID YOU NOT! Yes, people spread cowpats on their toast every morning to make the bread grow. That's how disgusting the countryside is!

"I AM NOT MOVING AND YOU CAN'T MAKE ME!" I said, this time in an EXTRA LOUD voice.

"I bet I *can* make you move, Maggie!" Mum said, and she tickled me – which obviously did make me move, even though I didn't want to. That was cheating and she knew it.

One thing you should know about my mum: she is NOT funny, but she thinks she is. So please do not laugh at *any* of her "jokes" because the more you laugh, the more she will tell, and nobody wants that. Especially not me, because this is *my* book and NOT my mum's.

There was only one thing for it. I would have to get Lily to help me.

"I am NOT moving to Knobbly Bottom," I told her. "I'm going to stay here and eat sweets for dinner every day instead. Are you with me, Lily?"

"You wanna play superheroes?" Lily replied.

One thing you should know about Lily: she *always* wants to play superheroes. Even when I'm in the middle of something super important like trying to stop our mum from ruining our LIVES.

"But superheroes don't live in Knobbly Bottom, Lily!" I said. "Everyone knows

8

superheroes live in Leicester. I saw Wonder Woman buying a sandwich in the big Tesco the other day."

"But Mummy said we can have ice cream with sprinkles on when we get to the new house," said Lily.

"My tongue will be much too sad to lick," I told her. "When tongues get sad they just go all floppy. I'll never lick an ice cream again and it'll be all your fault."

"Can I have yours then?" asked Lily.

I glared at her. "Fine, but I hope you like cow-poo-flavoured ice cream because that is the *only* kind they have in the countryside," I said.

I had never actually *eaten* a countryside ice

cream, but I was pretty sure they were made from hay and cowpats and yucky stuff like that.

Lily was no help at all, and Mum was still listening to absolutely none of my Good Reasons Not to Move to the Silly Old Countryside.

She was going on about how brilliant the new house would be because it has a garden, and that means I can play outside for the whole summer holiday. She even said I could have a horse to keep in it.

OK, so I did ask, "Can I have a horse? Can I have a horse? Can I have a horse?" about five hundred and ninety-eight zillion times and *refuse* to get into the car until she shouted, "Yes, whatever, Maggie!" But THAT IS STILL A YES.

She never did get me that horse, though. Because there's another thing you should know about my mum. She is a **big old liar**. In fact, I don't know how she sits down because her PANTS must be on fire ALL of the time.

Here are just a few of the dirty great whoppers she has told.

LIES MY MUM TELLS

1. I'm going without you!
   LIE.
   Everyone knows grown-ups are NOT allowed to leave children on their own ever or the grown-up will be sent to prison.

2. There are no more biscuits.
   TOTAL LIE.
   I once caught her scoffing a Hobnob in the kitchen after she told me there were none left, so when she says this

she actually means there are no more biscuits FOR MAGGIE.

3. If you don't clean your teeth twice a day they will all fall out.
COMPLETE LIE.
I once went TWO days without cleaning them and I still have all my teeth. (Well, apart from the baby ones I gave to the tooth fairy.)

4. There are no such things as monsters.
HUGE WHIPPITY WHOPPER OF A LIE.

In the end, even though I voted with TWO hands, all of my toes AND one sad tongue, we were moving to **Knobbly Bottom** and there was absolutely nothing I could do about it.

I suppose you are wondering why I haven't told you the **BIG SECRET** yet. Well, the thing about secrets as MASSIVE as this one is that you can't just blurt them out all at once. Not unless you want the person you are telling to totally **FREAK OUT!**

But don't worry because all will be revealed in the next chapter...

CHAPTER TWO

All is revealed...

NOT REALLY! What sort of book reveals everything in chapter two?! Not this one!

CHAPTER THREE

A bit is revealed but not everything as it's ONLY chapter three!

We had only lived in **Knobbly Bottom** for two days and I was already soooooooooooooooooooo oooooooooooooooooooooooooooooooooo bored.

The countryside was more boring than fractions or that TV show my mum watches where people cook dinner, then other people come and taste the dinner, and then they all stand around talking about the dinner.

There were NO soft play centres or toyshops or zebra crossings with pressy buttons like we had in Leicester! There was just one BORING church, one BORING shop, one BORING school that I will have to go to at the end of summer, and loads of stuff made from green.

There was basically **NOTHING** to do except look at fields of sheep, and everyone knows that sheep are the ~~BAA~~ringest animal ever invented. Also, my best friend Rav says you should never trust anything made of wool.

Anyway, I was about to die of boredom just for something to do, when a really weird thing happened!

It all started when Mum said we were going out to "explore". Although it turned out that "explore" actually meant "go to the village shop for milk".

Now you seem like a sensible sort of person. Well, let me ask you this. IF you saw THIS sign in a shop window, what would you do?

IMPORTANT NOTICE
No children or dogs.
INCLUDING:
Dogs who look like children.

Children who look like dogs (they're the worst ones).

So bog off or you will be gobbled up by

Gary the **Great** AND **Evil Child-Eater.**

Would you (a) take your precious children, one of which (Lily) could easily be mistaken for a small puppy, into the shop? Or would you (b) grab your children and run away from that shop as fast as your legs could carry you?

Well, my mum is *obviously* not a sensible sort of person because she only went and took me and Lily into that **SHOP OF HORRORS!!** It was almost like she *wanted* us to be gobbled up by a Great and Evil Child-Eater.

"Don't look so worried!" Mum said. "The sign is obviously a little joke! You always get quirky characters in the countryside. It's all part of the charm of a small village! Come on, girls." And with that, she grabbed our hands and *dragged* us into that shop like lambs to the slaughter! She may as well have covered us in ketchup and served us up to **Gary the Great and Evil Child-Eater** on a plate!

Luckily, when I saw **Gary the Great and Evil Child-Eater** I didn't feel quite as scared.

For a start, even though he was really tall, he didn't have any teeth, so I don't think he could eat a chicken drumstick, let alone a whole child! He looked very angry with my mum, though. Even when she gave him one of her super friendly smiles.

"Did yous not read the sign?" he snapped angrily. "The sign about the gobblement of childrens? Or maybe you is wanting your children to be gobbled up, mam. Is that it? Can't say I blames you."

"Oh yes, the sign! So funny!" My mum laughed. "Now where can I find the milk, please?"

At this point **Gary the Great and Evil Child-Eater** let out the LONGEST groan I have ever heard, before grumpily answering the question.

"UGHHHHH. Would that be cow milk, goat milk or the milk of a purple spotted unicorn?" he asked, which made my mum do one of her loud "pretend laughs".

"Just boring old cow's milk for us, please," she said.

"At the back. I'll shows you. Leave your ... *things* here," he said, pointing at me and Lily like we were pieces of dog poo, before taking my mum to find the milk.

One thing you should know about **Gary the Great and Evil Child-Eater** is that he is rubbish at shops. This was the worst shop I had ever been in! There were a few tins of beans, some boring-looking

magazines called things like *Farmer's Friend* and *Manure Monthly*, a sad selection of fruit and vegetables, and row upon row of jars filled with everything from what looked like dead insects to silver screws and cloudy water! Very weird.

While we were waiting for Mum, me and Lily thought we might as well see if we could find any sweets, in case Mum let us have something (it would be the least she could do for almost getting us gobbled up).

As we were hunting for them, a little old lady came into the shop. She wore a bright pink bobble hat on top of a head of thick, curly white hair, a long brown coat with loads of pockets, and dirty brown boots. She had red cheeks and twinkly blue eyes and was carrying the most enormous handbag I'd ever seen.

Now the thing about little old ladies is this: they can be very tricky.

"You like lollipops, duckalucks?" she said to us in a tricky old lady way, pulling a couple

of grubby-
looking green lollies
from her bag.

Then Lily got all excited
because she loves lollipops *and*
little old ladies, so she shouted, "Yes, please!"

Luckily for Lily, I knew all about **stranger danger** and **germs**, so I put a stop to the whole thing.

"No, thank you," I said to the old lady in my most grown-uppish voice. "We're not allowed to take lollies from strangers in case they kidnap us. And we're not allowed to eat dirty lollies in case they give us a tummy bug."

Now most *ordinary* little old ladies would have smiled and put the lollies away. They might even have told me how sensible I was for not taking sweets from strangers. But *not* this one.

THIS little old lady said something really, really odd.

"Be careful around here, girlies!" she warned, straightening her bright pink hat. "The countryside be a dangerous place for folks like you."

CHAPTER FOUR

A perfectly good plan
(if you ask me)

I was just about to tell the old lady that the countryside MIGHT be dangerous for people like Violet Parker, who are rubbish at climbing trees, but not for ME, when she said something even WEIRDER!

"Now was it bread I came in for or double-strength holy water? I can't remember for the life of me," she said.

"Look, if you're a stranger danger, I should tell you that I know Teenage Mutant Ninja Turtle," I said, doing my best ninja turtle pose. "*And* also our mummy is over there!"

"I'm off then. I wouldn't want to get on the

wrong side of a mummy!" she said, before winking at us and leaving the shop.

I told you old ladies were tricky.

Just then, my mum came over carrying a pint of milk.

"That lady told us the countryside is dangerous!" I said to her as she paid **Gary the Great and Evil Child-Eater** for the milk. "She said we should go back to Leicester!"

"Oh, really?" my mum said in a voice that meant she *definitely* didn't believe me.

"Yes! And she said she wanted to buy *holy water*, and then she…"

"What have I told you about making up stories, Maggie?" said my mum in her trying-not-to-shout-in-front-of-other-people voice.

I don't have a trying-not-to-shout-in-front-of-other-people voice, just a normal shout-in-front-of-other-people voice, which I used right there and then to tell my mum that I was going back to Leicester on my own right then because I missed our flat and I HATED **Knobbly Bottom** and everyone in it.

Then my mum started saying all this stuff about me to **Gary the Great and Evil Child-Eater** (who didn't look one bit interested, by the way) like, "She's having trouble settling into the new house", "She misses her friends", bla bla flipping bla.

When I started to get really upset, she asked if I wanted to choose a treat to cheer me up – SHUT me up more like!

I said I *would* like a treat but I would probably never be cheered up again, and if I got eaten by a shopkeeper or kidnapped by an old lady it would be all her fault.

Then Lily gave me a hug and told me she didn't want me to be eaten up, which made Mum go, "Aw,

how sweet! Lily, you can choose a treat too."
Five-year-olds are smarter than they look.

BUT telling me I could have "a treat" was another one of Mum's lies. When I picked up a chocolate bar, she said I could *only* have a healthy treat. So THEN I got some strawberry laces, which everyone knows are at least seventeen of your five a day, but she still said "NO".

It turned out that my mum *actually* meant that I could *only* have a treat made out of real fruit. So basically FRUIT. Well, to be more specific, an apple, because that's the only fruit they sold in the shop, and everyone (including my mum) knows that an APPLE is definitely NOT a treat, just a crunchy green ball of sadness.

"Thank you!" my mum said to a cross-looking Gary as she paid him for the shopping. "We'd better get back to the unpacking!"

"Oh, I wouldn't be bothering unpacking," said Gary, looking very serious. "Folk never stays in Knobbly Bottom for very long, see."

This made my mum do another one of her fake laughs, as if Gary had told her the funniest joke ever, instead of being the SECOND person to warn us about the countryside today!

It was when we finally left the creepy old shop that I came up with a BRILLIANT plan! A plan so BRILLIANT it would get me out of **Knobbly Bottom** AND make sure I had all the treats I wanted! I would go to stay with my BEST FRIEND Rav in Leicester! I can't believe I hadn't thought of it sooner, because on my last day at my old school, his mum had said I could come and stay ANY TIME I LIKED.

So I realized I could probably just go and stay with them until I was eighteen (old enough to get my own flat), and that way I'd never have to go back to **Knobbly Bottom** ever again! Simple!

And the best bit was, Rav has a cupboard in his kitchen FULL of treats (which has no apples in it, by the way).

Plus, they have lemonade and Coke and sometimes his mum even lets us have sweets BEFORE and AFTER dinner. Mum says this is why Rav has five fillings and I have none. Although when I told Rav this, he said he would rather have fillings and sweets than no fillings and no sweets. He's always saying clever stuff like that. He's the smartest person I know. He can even do times tables without using his fingers.

I couldn't wait to go and stay with him! There was just one problem: my mum.

"I don't think Rav's mum meant you could

visit them for nine years, Maggie," she said when I brought up my plan later.

"They didn't say I *couldn't* visit for nine years," I told her.

"Yes, but when people say 'come and stay' they mean for a day or two, not for almost a decade!"

"But how do you *know* that?" I yelled.

Then she said, "I just do," which is basically what grown-ups say when they don't know the answer to something.

So anyway, I wasn't allowed to "invite myself to Rav's for the rest of my childhood", but Mum said she would arrange for us to go and visit them for a day "once we're settled in" – IF I stopped going on about it.

But it's OK, because I know that when I tell Rav and his parents all about creepy old **Knobbly Bottom**, they'll probably come and rescue me themselves! Until then, I decided that the sensible thing to do would be to stay away from EVERYONE and EVERYTHING in this weird village.

And so I did.

Or I *tried* to.

But then I met a burglar called Fred.

CHAPTER FIVE

A burglar called Fred

I first met Fred when me and Lily were playing "stop the ball going over next door's fence", but Lily wasn't very good, so it went over the fence.

"Lily! You are supposed to *stop* it going over! That is the whole point of the game!" I moaned, just as the ball came flying back over the fence and hit me on the head.

"Sorry!" shouted a boy with curly hair wearing an army-green bandana and full-

camouflage clothes. He was standing, looking very suspicious, in next door's garden.

Now I *knew* for a fact that an old man called Mr Tibble lived in the house next door and *not* a boy wearing camouflage clothes. I knew this because when we first moved in, he gave us some courgettes he had grown in his garden, and even though Mum, Lily and me HATE courgettes (they are basically evil cucumbers), Mum said "oh lovely", so the next day he brought us some MORE. So we had only been in **Knobbly Bottom** for ONE week and already had nine courgettes in our fridge, which is a bit much if you ask me. Especially because Mum is now saying we have to eat them to "be polite". This would never happen in Leicester.

"Are you a burglar?" I asked the boy. "Because that is not your house, so that is not your garden."

"No, I'm Fred," he replied.

"Fred the thief?" I suggested.

"I'm nine years old! Burglars are way older than that!" He laughed.

So then *I* said that burglars might send a nine-year-old boy called Fred into the back garden to distract the neighbours while the rest of the gang snuck into the house and nicked all the stuff.

I thought this was a very good point, but the boy had the cheek to ask me if *I* was a burglar, seeing as I knew so much about burgling.

"I am not a burglar!" I told him. "I live here!"

"Ha! That's exactly what a burglar would say!" he replied.

"Aha!" I cried. "How would you know what a burglar would say unless *you* were a burglar?"

Then, while we were arguing about which one of us was a burglar, Lily only blimming went and kicked the ball over the fence again. And the next thing I knew, Burglar Boy picked up our ball, jumped over the fence into OUR GARDEN and gave it back to Lily.

Then Lily started kicking the ball back and forth with him like everything was fine!

"Lily!" I shouted. "Stop playing football with *him*. And Burglar Boy, get out of our garden *right now!*"

"I'm not a burglar!" said Fred again. "My granddad is Mr Tibble, and I've just moved in with him actually."

"So *YOU* say!" I snapped. "Now go away or,

or I'll, err…"

"She'll zap you with her Mega-Blaster." Lily smiled, handing me a stick.

"Exactly!" I agreed, holding up the stick in a tough, superhero-type way.

Then the little traitor shouted, "Let's play superheroes with Fred!" and gave Burglar Boy a stick too. A **BIGGER** one than mine.

Another thing you should know about Lily

is that "playing superheroes" is basically just pretend-hitting each other with sticks, pillows, balloons, or anything you can get your hands on. So if you don't like being pretend-hit with stuff, don't EVER play superheroes with Lily.

Luckily, I do like playing superheroes, and I managed to zap Fred three times with my Mega-Blaster before he got away. We dodged Lily when she tried to get us with her Taser Twig, but then Fred hit me with three Deadly Dandelion Bombs and so I was out.

"Fred for the win! Whoop!" yelled Fred triumphantly. "My dad is actually a real-life superhero, so that's why I'm so good at this game!"

"Ha! There are no superheroes in Knobbly Bottom," I said, a bit annoyed about losing to a boy who may or may not be a burglar. "Unless he's called Captain Bottom! Does he drive a Bottom-Mobile?"

"Nope, but he has got a secret lair! Come with me. I'll show you," said Fred, and he beckoned us to follow him over the fence and into his granddad's garden.

He led us to a gigantic shed that took up at least half of the lawn, and pulled open the door. Inside, there were boxes of all shapes and sizes piled right up to the ceiling.

"What is all this stuff?" I asked as Lily pulled a big pair of binoculars out of a box.

"Superhero kit, obviously." Fred smiled as he opened a box full of military uniforms, utility belts and hats. "My dad is in the army!"

Superhero Kit

"Cool," I said, pulling on a camouflage vest that had about one million pockets.

It turned out that Fred had moved in with his granddad, Mr Tibble, while his dad was away doing lots of dangerous missions and stuff. Fred said he didn't mind at all because his granddad always had loads of boiled sweets and biscuits.

Then Lily yelled something about round two of the **Knobbly Bottom Superhero Battle**, and so Fred and I grabbed our Mega-Blasters and ran outside!

Suddenly, I was accidentally having the most fun I'd had since moving to **Knobbly Bottom**.

In fact, I was having such a nice time I almost forgot about weird, child-eating shopkeepers and tricky old ladies and their warnings.

But I should remind you that this is a **SCARY STORY** and when people have a brilliant time in a **SCARY STORY** it usually means things are about to go very, very wrong...

CHAPTER SIX

Red eyes at night are NOT anyone's delight actually

LIES MY MUM TOLD ME ABOUT THE COUNTRYSIDE

1. It is peaceful.
   LIE!
   There might not be any traffic sounds
   or sirens like there were in Leicester,
   but the countryside is full to the brim
   of NOISE. Cows constantly mooing like
   rascals at all hours of the day and
   night. Sheep baa-ing away to each
   other about the weather (probably),
   cockerels cock-a-doodle-dooing and
   birds singing their heads off at FIVE

o'clock in the morning. What the heck do they have to be so happy about at five o'clock in the morning? Peaceful it is not! Give me the sound of roaring city roads over a growling combine harvester any day!

2. **The air is cleaner.**
ANOTHER LIE!
As I have already mentioned, it smells of poo. How can something that smells of poo be clean? We are literally inhaling cow-bum juice.

3. **It is more friendly than the city.**
TOTAL LIE!
I never met an evil child-eating Gary in the big Tesco or a tricky old lady in McDonald's.

4. It is safer.
   ABSOLUTE SMACKATTACK OF A
   LIE. One of the first things I noticed
   when we moved to Knobbly Bottom was
   how DARK it is at night! You could
   trip over a stile or slip on a cowpat and
   break your arm, for goodness' sake.

In Leicester, there were always loads of lamp posts and car headlights so it never looked SUPER PITCH-BLACK like it does in **Knobbly Bottom**.

The sky is sooooo black here you can see all the stars – which FYI do not make much light at all! How on earth did those shepherds from the Bible find their way to baby Jesus following just one star? I did ask my teacher Mrs Olsen about this when we did the nativity last year at my old school, but all she said was, "They just did". Classic grown-up reply to a question they don't know the answer to.

So, if you think about it, the countryside is NOT safer at all, because everyone knows that dangerous stuff happens in the dark.

BUT if it hadn't been for this super pitch-darkness, I might not have noticed a pair of **GLOWING RED EYES OF DOOM** out of my bedroom window.

After playing outside with Fred and Lily until late o'clock, Mum said I had to turn my light off straight away, which I said was a silly idea because then I wouldn't be able to see my book. But according to my mum it was too late to read. The thing is, according to me it was a perfectly good time to read, so I was planning to find my torch and read under the covers as soon as I heard her go downstairs. And this was exactly what I was doing when I heard a really loud noise coming from outside.

At first I thought it was someone shouting "RAAR" in a loud voice, but then I realized it was "~~BAA~~". A silly old sheep was out there

44

bleating at the top of its voice! How rude! If it was too late to read, it was definitely too late to "BAA" your head off. So I ran to the window, pulled back my curtains and saw the biggest, woolliest and scariest-looking sheep standing in the field at the end of my garden!

And it looked right up at me with its **GLOWING RED EYES!**

I know what you are thinking. *"Maggie, you must have been dreaming!"*

Well, I am sorry to tell you this, but I was

WIDE awake, and the sheep's eyes were definitely BLOOD-COLOURED, which is why I had NO choice but to go and investigate! Despite the fact it was night, aka the **Time When Dangerous Stuff Happens**.

I put on my dressing gown and slippers and slid my torch into my pocket. Then I tiptoed out of my bedroom, only to come face to face with a...

"LILY!" I said.

"Where are you going?" she whispered.

"I'm on a secret mission that is MUCH too scary for five-year-olds," I told her. "Now go back to your room or I'll tell Mummy you aren't in bed!"

"Are you going to tell her that *you* aren't in bed too?" said Lily.

UGH! Little sisters are so annoying. Especially when you're trying to investigate suspicious sheep. She REFUSED to go back to bed, so I had no choice but to take her with me before Mum heard her making a racket.

"OK. Just stay behind me and be super quiet!" I said firmly as we snuck down the stairs. "And if a massive sheep with red eyes comes near us, run!"

Luckily, my mum was too busy watching another boring TV show – where people have their houses decorated and then cry about it – to notice me and Lily creeping into the kitchen and quietly out the back door.

We tiptoed down the garden path, and *that* is when we saw a dark figure standing silently at the end of the garden.

It had pointy ears and a HUGE head, with a fierce-looking alligator snout. Lily grabbed hold of my hand tightly and we were just about to make a super-quick RETREAT when the creature spoke…

"Maggie? Lily?" The voice in the darkness was familiar.

I fished my torch out of my dressing-gown pocket and pointed it at the BEAST – which began walking towards me!

"Ow! Stop shining that thing in my eyes!" said the beast, which wasn't a beast at all. It was Fred the Burglar Boy in a dinosaur onesie!

"What are you doing in our garden at night?" I hissed. "Perhaps you are a burglar after all?"

"I'm patrolling the area actually," he said, holding up a big pair of binoculars and a wooden spoon. "My dad says that in the army you should NEVER go to sleep until you've checked your base for danger and had a big hot chocolate."

"But this is *my* base, not yours, and I am patrolling it myself, thank you very much! And why have you got a wooden spoon?" I asked him.

"First rule of army training: always carry a wooden spoon," he said proudly.

"Really?"

"Yep. Anyway, you should be thanking me – I just scared off a very angry-looking sheep that was trying to get through your back gate!" said Fred, pointing his spoon in the direction of the field where I had seen the **Glowing Red Eyes of Doom**.

"Did it have red eyes?" I asked him.

"I suppose they did look a bit sore, now you mention it," said Fred.

"And evil?"

"More like hayfever?" said Fred. "Or perhaps it had been crying?"

"Sheep don't cry!" I said.

But Fred said they might if they were allergic

to wool or scared of the dark or something. Then Lily started tugging at my dressing gown.

"Maggie, look! Red stars!" she said, pointing over the back fence into the darkness beyond.

But it wasn't red stars she had seen. It was the **Glowing Red Eyes of Doom!**

"They're not stars, Lily!" I said. "Fred, have a look through the binoculars!"

I shone my torch across the field, while Fred held the binoculars to his eyes and his jaw dropped.

"What do you see?" I asked impatiently. "Let me look!"

"Subject is larger than average. White wool, a black nose, red eyes, four legs. Standing in a large field to the west of Knobbly Bottom."

"What?" I said, grabbing the binoculars from Fred.

There it was – the huge sheep with weird eyes and what looked like sharp white fangs! "It's the red-eyed sheep! I knew it!"

"That's exactly what I said!" said Fred.

"That is no ordinary sheep, though," I said. "Ordinary sheep don't have evil red eyes and pointy teeth! It's like some sort of … VAMPIRE SHEEP!"

But before we could take another look, the patio light flicked on and a dark shadow was cast over the lawn.

"What on EARTH are you doing out here?" It was my mum, standing outside the back door looking very cross. "You are supposed to be in bed!"

"But look in the field," I said. "It's a vampire sheep!"

But the sheep had vanished, so all Mum saw was Fred standing at the end of the garden in his dinosaur onesie.

"Good evening, Fred," she said. "Now I expect your granddad will want you back in bed too. It's far too late to play outside."

Then, even though we all tried to tell her

about the Red-eyed Sheep Vampire Monster Thing, she was having none of it. You can't talk to Mum about anything when she's decided it's bedtime.

But the thing about Red-eyed Sheep Vampire Monster Things is this: they always come back.

CHAPTER SEVEN

What if the boy who cried wolf WAS telling the truth?

I know what you're thinking. *"Maggie is a big liar because my parents told me there's no such thing as monsters."*

Well, I hate to tell you this, but your parents are fibbers just like my mum. In fact, a grown-up's most favourite lie to tell children is that monsters do NOT exist.

I expect you are also thinking that monsters are creatures whose eyes are orange and tongues are black, with purple prickles all over their backs, but you are wrong because that's a Gruffalo and he is a book monster and definitely not real.

Well, I have discovered that REAL monsters

come in all different shapes and sizes and flavours just like humans. Some are big, some are small and some look like SCARY VAMPIRE SHEEP! And I was about to make another discovery about them.

And it happened the VERY next day, when Mum told me and Lily to go in the back garden to "get some fresh air".

My mum is obsessed with "fresh air" (almost as much as she is with vegetables and teeth-cleaning) so even though we were having a perfectly nice time being bored *inside*, we had to go and be bored outside in a garden that doesn't have a horse in it because Mum says they're too expensive. If you ask me, it's a total waste of a garden *not* to have a pet in it. I even tried to persuade her to let me have a rat because I know I can get one from a sewer for FREE, but she wouldn't let me have one of those, either.

Anyway, me and Lily had decided to play hide-and-squirt (basically like hide-and-seek but when you find the hider you squirt them with your water pistol), so I was crouching underneath a bush when I heard some deep voices coming from the field behind our garden! They sounded so creepy they made my ears want to crawl off my head and bury themselves in the mud.

Luckily, I am the boss of my ears so instead I peeped over the bush to find out who the heckedy-doo-dah was making that noise!

Was it a cow with a sore throat? Some creepy farmers on a picnic? Nope. It was some SHEEP HAVING A CHAT!

"WAIT? WHAT?" you are probably thinking. *"Sheep don't have chats!"*

What is going on? I thought.

"GO ~~BAA~~WAY!" shouted the biggest sheep, who had spotted me peering over the bush at him. "SCRAM, KIDDO. GET OUTTA HERE."

BUT he didn't say it in Sheep, he said it in *Human*! That was when I realized it was the big,

red-eyed vampire sheep from the other night.
But this time he had three red-eyed vampire
sheep mates with him!

Now I don't know about you, but I had
NEVER EVER heard a vampire sheep speak
Human English before, so I must have gone
into shock because I tried to talk while trying
not to talk (if you're not supposed to talk to

strangers, surely you're doubly not supposed to talk to strangers who are also talking vampire sheep).

"W-w-whattheflipwhoareyou?" I mumbled.

"I said, BAA-BAA-be gone, you dirty braaat!" replied the horrible creature, flashing his sharp fangs at me.

Then before I got the chance to say something super clever like "GO AWAY YOURSELF, YOU WOOLLY WALLY!", Lily found me.

"Found you! I win!" she cried, chasing me out of my hiding place with her TURBO 300 Super Soaker.

"LILY!" I said. "Did you hear that sheep talk to me?"

"What sheep?" asked Lily.

"There!" I pointed over the fence only to find the gang of sheep had gone. They must have trotted off across the field.

"Is it an invisible sheep?" Lily asked. "Because I can *definitely* see an invisible sheep."

"You can't see invisible things, Lily. That's the whole point of them!" I explained, but Lily just shrugged.

Then I ran inside to tell my mum, because I might be the hero of this story, but I *am* only nine and I had just been shouted at by a very mean vampire sheep.

"Mum, can sheep talk? Because a big sheep with red eyes and sharp teeth just shouted at me!" I said in a panic.

"I don't know, Maggie," Mum said. "Was this 'talking sheep' anything like the talking cow you saw the other day who told you to MOOve back to Leicester, or else?'"

"No, but…"

"Or was it more like the horse who said we do not want new NEIGH-bours in Knobbly Bottom?"

This was so annoying! Now I knew how that boy who cried wolf felt. I bet *he* only made up stories about wolves to try and escape from the stinking countryside.

"I double promise you *this* is NOT a story!" I yelled. "The scary vampire sheep really and truly spoke to me in real life!"

Then, before I could say anything else, Lily rushed in and told Mum that we had seen an invisible sheep in the garden. This made it sound like I had TOTALLY made it up! And you will NOT believe what Mum said to Lily.

"Aw, that's nice, love!"

The flipping cheek of it! So she *believed* Lily saw an invisible sheep, even though *everyone* knows you can't see invisible things, because THAT IS THE POINT OF THEM, but she wouldn't believe ME about a visible sheep speaking to *me* in Human? It was so unfair.

That's when I told her I was going to call the police to ask them to investigate an evil gang of talking vampire sheep.

But Mum said the police have more important things to do than "listen to my stories" so I wasn't allowed to phone them! What could be more important than a vampire sheep?! An *evil* vampire sheep who would be very pleased to know that the police had "better things to do" than stop them from TERRIFYING children in their own gardens!

So that was when I decided I had NO choice. I would have to find out what was going on in **Knobbly Bottom** (not, I repeat, an actual knobbly bum – that would be gross!) all by myself.

CHAPTER EIGHT

Baa baa beast sheep

The problem with trying to investigate stuff when you are nine is that you're not allowed to go out on your own. And the problem with not being allowed to go out on your own is that you have to find other ways to investigate, which might get you banned from biscuits for a week.

Although, in my opinion, if anyone should be banned from biscuits it should be my mum! If she hadn't made us move to **Knobbly Bottom** in the first place, I wouldn't have ended up having to *do* what I did.

None of it was my fault really. It would have been an AMAZING plan if it had worked.

On the day of my amazing plan, my mum was having her morning shower. She has a shower *every single morning,* which is a bit much if you ask me. I don't know how she gets so dirty while she's asleep. Anyway, she is always in there for two episodes of our favourite cartoon. This means me and Lily have exactly twenty-six minutes of parent-free time, which we normally use to sneak some biscuits out of the tin. One of us will keep watch for Mum at the bottom of the stairs, while the other one grabs a few Hobnobs and brings them back to base (the settee). Then we scoff them before Mum comes down and starts nagging us to get dressed.

Well, I was at the Grab and Run stage of Operation Biscuits when I saw something out of the kitchen window that made me forget all about Hobnobs.

Yep, you guessed it! The strange vampire sheep were BACK in the field at the end of our garden! There were even more of them now, and they were looking very much like they were **UP TO NO GOOD.** They were walking towards a large barn at the other side of the field, their razor-sharp fangs glistening in the morning sunlight.

I *had* to get my mum! This was my big chance to PROVE to her once and for all that red-eyed vampire sheep did exist and so we should definitely go back to Leicester!

But the problem with mums when they are in the shower is this: they don't want to get out. So when I shouted up the stairs that she needed to come down RIGHT NOW because there was a **VAMPIRE SHEEP EMERGENCY**, she just said "in a minute", and everyone knows that grown-up minutes last THREE HOURS.

That was why I had NO choice but to do the thing that got me banned from biscuits.

I thought if I could get a VIDEO of these vampire sheep on my mum's phone, she would HAVE to believe me. So I grabbed her mobile off the sideboard and headed for the back door!

"Where are you going?" Lily said as soon as I opened the door. "Why have you got Mummy's phone?"

"Shush! I'm going on another secret mission

and I need the camera, but you can't tell Mum!" I whispered to her. "Go back inside!"

"Oh, I'm coming too," she said, wrapping her dressing gown around her shoulders like a cape. "Super Lily to the rescue!"

I didn't have time to argue, so we ran out the back door, through the little gate at the end of our garden and into the field. There were even more of the woolly beasts heading for the barn now – all different shapes and sizes. Some were small and lamb-like and some were tall or round, but they *all* had the same evil red eyes. When they reached the big barn, they piled inside and so we had NO choice but to follow them.

We found a small door around the back of the big building and gently pushed it open. Luckily, the vampire sheep were too busy ~~BAA~~-ing among themselves to notice us sneak in and dive in between some massive bales of hay. For once I was very glad to be small (and good at hiding).

I had just taken my mum's phone out of my pocket and pressed record when we heard a creepy sound, like a BAA-gone-wrong, echo across the big barn.

"BAAFACE!   BAAFACE!   BAAFACE!!" cheered the vampire sheep.

I carefully peeped over the hay bale, and there he was – the ginormous sheep who had shouted at me in my garden! He was standing on a stage made from stacked hay bales! He must be called BAAface. Today he wore dark sunglasses and looked very, very pleased with himself.

"TELL US THE PLAN, MIGHTY BAAFACE!" the crowd of vampire sheep yelled at their leader.

"OK, fellas and fellettes. Listen up. Our plan to take over the world and other evil stuff is officially on!" he announced, nodding towards a map of **Knobbly Bottom** stuck to the wall next to him. "First, we need an army! This map says there are three farms right here in the village! We go in, turn every sheep we find into a vampire, until we have our very own fearsome flock. BAA-Da-Bing, fellas!"

"BAA-Da-Boom," replied the other vampire sheep, bowing to BAAface.

"And we will not stop there, my friends. Once we have taken over the village, we take on the WORLD! And then we'll be in charge, and those wool-less, blunt-toothed HUMANS will be the ones living in fields and eating nothing but grass!" shouted BAAface before bursting into evil laughter. All the vampire sheep cheered!

And that is when my AMAZING plan went VERY, VERY wrong…

"I NEED A POO POO!" said Lily. *Seriously?* Little sisters have terrible timing!

"You'll have to hold it in, Lily!" I whisper-shouted, hoping that the vampire sheep wouldn't hear us. "I told you not to come with me! Now shush!"

"But I *really, really* need a poo poo, Maggie!" said Lily, loudly enough for ~~BAA~~face to hear!

I tried my best to blend into the hay bales, but it was too late. He turned his head and glared right at us! "WHO ~~BAAA~~ YOU, AND WHAT'S THIS ABOUT POO?" he growled.

"Uh-oh!" I grabbed Lily's hand, scrambled to my feet, and headed for the door, dragging her behind me.

Then, just when we thought things couldn't get any worse, the door turned out to be JAMMED. I pushed as hard as I could, but it was stuck tight and the vampire sheep were coming towards us, looking very cross indeed. We were trapped!

"Oh no!" I cried, rattling the door handle again, but it wouldn't budge.

Suddenly there was a loud whistle from the other side of the barn.

The vampire sheep froze and went completely silent. And just when you thought this story couldn't get any weirder, I looked round to see the LITTLE OLD LADY from the shop standing on top of a really high stack of hay bales.

"Morning, duckalucks!" she shouted over to me and Lily. "Do you girls know the most important rule of the countryside?"

We didn't know what else to do but shake our heads, trying not to look at the gang of vampire sheep just metres away from us.

"Never play cards with a cow!" said the old lady. "No, wait, that's not it. Although you really shouldn't – they cheat, see. Always carry a spare chicken? Never be rude to a cowpat? Nope, it's not that one neither."

At this point, the gruesome vampire sheep, who had stopped to see what this strange old lady was on about, must have got bored because they started heading towards us again. I kicked the door as hard as I could, but it was still stuck fast!

"WAIT! I gots it!"

I looked back and the old lady smiled, pulling what looked like a leaf blower out of her huge handbag and aiming it at the jammed door.

"Never leave the house without a SUPERSONIC DOOR-BLOWER-OFFER! Stand back, girls!"

She winked at me and Lily as we backed away from the door, then she flicked a switch on her leaf blower and a HUGE gust of wind shot across the barn – and blew the back door right off its hinges! The blast was so powerful it blew entire hay bales across the barn AND my

mum's phone right out of my hand! This was
clearly no ordinary leaf blower.

"Now get out of here, duckalucks!" the old

lady yelled – and we RAN out of the barn as fast as our legs could carry us.

But it wasn't until we got halfway across the field that we saw the **SCARIEST THING OF ALL.**

CHAPTER NINE

More than we BAArgained for...

Outside the barn, wearing a bright blue flowery dressing gown and a towel on her head, was **The Most Terrifying Thing of All.**

"I HAVE BEEN WORRIED SICK. YOU COULD HAVE BEEN KIDNAPPED OR TRAMPLED BY A COW OR RUN OVER BY A TRACTOR. YOU ARE NEVER LEAVING THE HOUSE AGAIN. I HAVE CALLED THE POLICE AND THEY ARE GOING TO BE VERY CROSS WITH

YOU!" my mum shouted without stopping for breath.

It turned out she hadn't *really* called the police (another lie for her collection!), but our next-door neighbour, Mr Tibble, had told her he had seen me and Lily in the field in our pyjamas when he was walking his dog. What a tell-tale tit!

So my mum ran all the way there in her dressing gown and slippers. That's how much she wanted to shout at us!

When we got back inside, she said I was grounded for a whole month, but I told her I was glad about that because I didn't want to go out in this rubbish village anyway. And *that* was when she banned me from biscuits for a week.

You have probably already guessed that my mum did NOT believe me about ~~BAA~~face and the other sheep having an "evil plan meeting" in the barn. Or about the old lady blasting her Door-Blower-Offer. Even though Lily said she saw it all too, my mum said she was just going along with my "silly stories". The cheek of it!

And get this! EVERYTHING I filmed on my mum's phone had been deleted and replaced with five minutes of my chin. Mum says this was because I had it on "selfie mode" so it was facing me the whole time, but it was obviously some sort of vampire magic.

Then she said that there was bound to be a **Perfectly Logical Explanation** for everything that had happened. A perfectly logical explanation basically means what my mum *thinks* happened and not what *actually* happened.

My Mum's Perfectly Logical Explanation

Mum said when she went back to the barn to get her mobile phone she saw absolutely no vampire sheep or old ladies whatsoever. (Also, I am now banned from touching her phone ever again because it blew into some sheep poo. So really it's the sheep who should be banned from using it, not me.)

Mum said that sometimes animals do make human-like noises, which must have been what I'd heard because sheep definitely can't speak Human English.

And can you believe she *even* had a **Perfectly Logical Explanation** for the old lady from the shop who blasted open an ACTUAL door with a super-powered leaf blower!

"The door was probably blown open by the wind! Look, you get some very unusual characters in the countryside, Maggie! Your old lady is probably just a bit eccentric!" (Eccentric is grown-up speak for MASSIVE WEIRDO.)

She went on about these "explanations" (lies) soooooo much that she ALMOST had me believing them. Mums are sneaky like that. They know how to get into your head. Plus, she said if I stopped going on about vampire sheep and evil plans she might un-ban me from biscuits.

So I did. Until I remembered that Fred's dad was a soldier! If anyone could rescue us from a flock of evil sheep, surely it was those guys! That was literally the whole point of the army.

So the next day, I found Fred kicking a ball around in his garden and told him all about the talking sheep and their plan to take over the world.

"Are you sure the sheep were speaking?" asked Fred in a suspicious voice. "Just seems a bit funny because, well, animals can't talk, can they?"

"It *was* a bit funny, Fred! That's what I am trying to tell you! YOU saw them. They had red eyes and fangs."

"My granddad told me you get all different sorts of sheep," said Fred. "Maybe those ones are a rare breed like a Swaledale or the lesser-known Badger-Face Mountain Sheep?"

"Well, do any of those breeds wear SUNGLASSES, Fred?" I snapped. "The big leader sheep was wearing huge dark ones!"

"Sheep do not wear sunglasses, Maggie."

"Vampire sheep might, though, because everyone knows vampires hate the sun!" I told him. "He must have stolen them off an unsuspecting farmer!"

"Vampires? Look, if you're trying to scare me it won't work!" said Fred. "My dad said the second rule of army training is: never be afraid of too much butter…"

"What? Who'd be afraid of butter?" I asked.

"Butter, sheep, enemy nations…" mumbled Fred. "The point is, I'm not afraid!"

"Well, you should be! Something is NOT right. We really need to tell your dad about this so he can get the army to come and save us. Maybe he can bring a few tanks!" I said.

Then Fred said that even if they *were* vampire sheep, his dad wouldn't be able to get the whole army to **Knobbly Bottom** without any PROOF. He said I would need to get photographs or videos and that sort of thing. But of course my mum had banned me from her phone.

Luckily, Fred said his granddad had a camera without a phone on it (old people are weird), and that we could borrow it to get EVIDENCE of these "so-called vampire sheep".

"Great!" I said. "Bring on Operation Gather Evidence for the Army!"

Then Fred went and got the camera, and I found a notebook to write down any Important Information. We asked Lily to find some Beast Blasters (big twigs), and then we all waited at the end of the garden for the sheep to appear.

We waited and waited and then waited some more.

And we saw loads and loads of NOTHING. Not one single sheep. They were obviously hiding because they knew we were ON TO THEM.

Right about now, I expect you are thinking that my mum was right and I probably am the kind of girl who makes up stories about evil vampire sheep. Well, that is very rude indeed because I'm definitely NOT.

And if you're not thinking *that*, I BET you're thinking that this is going be one of those books where there ACTUALLY IS a **Perfectly Logical Explanation** for everything!

Like, it was ALL a bad dream, or the vampire sheep were just people in vampire sheep costumes.

Maybe you are secretly hoping that it *will* be that kind of book because that would be much less terrifying.

Well, I'm afraid that this is NOT one of those books.

Everything I've told you is absolutely true with a cherry on top, including the fact that **Knobbly Bottom** was full to the brim of woolly, fanged beasts. I just had to prove it.

BUT don't worry. If you're too scared to hear any more about the real-life VAMPIRE SHEEP, then here is a picture of a delicious apple pie you can look at until the end of the story instead. Unless you're scared of apple pies. In which case, I'll meet you in the next chapter.

CHAPTER TEN

Things get even more BAArmy

The next morning, Mum told me and Lily to get dressed because we were going to do something "fun".

At first, I didn't get too excited because what my mum says is fun and what is ACTUALLY fun are sometimes VERY different things.

Like the other day she said there was something "really fun" for me and Lily in the dining room. So we ran down the stairs and into the dining room as fast as we could and do you know what we found? Empty boxes! She had unpacked three of the big moving boxes and thought we might like to play with them.

I told her that unless there was a horse or a

pet rat in one of them, I did NOT want to play with cardboard boxes.

(As it happens, we did end up making a SPACESHIP and a CASTLE and a CASTLE SPACESHIP out of the boxes, which was fun, but do NOT tell my mum.)

Then sometimes she says we are going to do something "fun" and we go for a walk! Not even a walk TO anywhere, just a walk! Which is a waste of legs if you ask me.

"We are off to the Knobbly Bottom event

of the year!" said Mum, waving around a flyer that said *Knobbly Bottom Event of the Year* in big bubble writing. "The church fete!"

"Will there be a big wheel and dodgems?" I asked hopefully. "Or a ghost train?"

"No, but it says here there will be a tombola and welly wanging!" Mum said, handing me the flyer.

"What the heck-a-doo-dah is welly wanging?" I asked.

"You throw a welly boot as far as you can across a field!" my mum replied.

"Why?" I asked.

"Because it's fun."

At this point, I think my mum was realizing that this sounded totally CRUDICULOUS, so she told us there would also be an ice-cream van and a cake stall.

"But I don't want a cowpat ice cream," said Lily.

"There'll be loads of flavours, Lily. Come on,

it'll be a good way to get to know people in the village," said Mum.

I suppose it was better than boxes.

So that was why we ended up at the church that Sunday morning instead of watching cartoons in our pyjamas like we normally did. But I figured it might give me the chance to sneak off and see if I could find out anything else about the sheep. I had even taken my Super Soaker just in case things got dangerous.

When we got to the churchyard, there were balloons and bunting everywhere. Unfortunately, there were NO fairground rides, but there was a small bouncy castle, an ice-cream van as promised, and tables full of delicious-looking cakes and sweets.

Fred's granddad, Mr Tibble, stood next to a pile of old wellies, and if you gave him 50p you could throw one. Or for 20p you could try and knock a coconut off a stick, or you could pay a pound to win a tin of beans or a dusty bottle

of cider on the tombola. There was also a tent with a sign on it that said *The Great Bottom Bake Off*, which apparently wasn't a bum-cooking competition, but the **Knobbly Bottom** annual baking contest.

Anyway, so far so BORING! Then I had an idea. The church was surrounded by farmland! And where there were farms there might just be VAMPIRE SHEEP!

"Do you want to play superheroes?" I asked Lily, while Mum was busy having a go on the tombola. "Today's top-secret mission is to find those scary vampire sheep!"

"Oh, can I keep one?" said Lily. "I've always wanted a vampire sheep."

"No, you can't! They're very dangerous, Lily!" I said firmly. "IF we spot one, we will just follow it from a distance and find out what it is up to! But you must NOT go near them because they might bite!"

"OK," said Lily.

But then Mum came over
and made us go and look
at Mr Tibble's wellies.

"I was a champion
wanger back in my
day, see. Tibble the
Wanger they called
me. I once threw a
left size eleven so
far it ended up in the
next village!" he said proudly.

Then my mum asked me if I wanted to a
"wang a welly" and you will not believe what
happened next! I said NO I definitely did NOT
want to, but she made me have a go anyway! I
don't know why she even bothered *asking* me in
the first place. It's like when she asks if I *want*
to wash my hair, and when I say no (because
hair doesn't get dirty just sitting on my head all
day), SHE MAKES ME WASH IT ANYWAY!

So then I got really cross with her and

chucked a blue welly REALLY hard without properly looking. The next thing I knew, it had bounced right through the door of the Great Bottom Bake Off tent and landed smack-bang in the middle of a Victoria sponge.

Then my mum told ME off, even though it was HER fault for making me wang a welly in the first place! She told me to look after Lily while she went to apologize to a cross-looking lady covered in jam and cream.

The first thing me and Lily did was go to the sweet stall. We decided we needed lots of energy sweets for our secret sheep-seeking mission.

You would not believe how many sweets they had. Chocolate bars, lollipops, jelly babies and even sherbet dips! We bought two packets of jelly babies, a sherbet dip and two chocolate bars just to be on the safe side.

We were just opening them when Fred came running over to us with his granddad's big old camera on a strap around his neck.

"Wow, you must be hungry," he said, looking at our sweets.

"We're on a top-secret mission so we need lots of energy actually," I told him.

"If it was *that* top secret you shouldn't have mentioned it in the first place," said Fred. "That's the most important rule of top-secret missions."

Then I said I only told him because me and Lily were going to find the vampire sheep so we needed him to take photos for Evidence. "I'm in," said Fred, giving us a little salute. "I might need some energy sweets first, though!"

So I gave him a chocolate bar and we decided we should go and search the GRAVEYARD first, because everyone knows that is an evil baddie's favourite place to hang out. Plus, Fred said there was a farm behind it.

I know what you're thinking. *"Graveyards are PETRIFYING! Nothing good ever happens in a graveyard. Don't do it, Maggie!"*

Well, luckily I am super brave and graveyards don't scare me one little bit. After all, everyone who lives there is dead and dead people can't be dangerous.

We walked right to the very end of the graveyard until we came to an old stone wall. And over the stone wall was a meadow filled with green trees, beautiful buttercups and SHEEP! At last, we would be able to get evidence of the **EVIL VAMPIRE SHEEP OF DOOM** to send to Fred's dad. Then the army would jump in their tanks straight away!

"There they are!" I said, pointing across the meadow.

Three sheep were munching on grass greedily, but they had their backs to us, so they just looked like ordinary sheep. Luckily, I had an idea.

"OI, FANG FEATURES!" I yelled across the field.

"The VAMPIRE SHEEP!" muttered Fred, his mouth wide open in shock as the sheep turned to look at us with their rotten red eyes. "But I thought vampires couldn't go out in the sun?"

"Well, I don't make the rules, Fred. Their wool must protect them from the sun's rays! Now quickly take some photos!" I gasped as the vampire sheep started trotting our way. "We'd better get out of here!"

Then I turned round to grab Lily's hand – and that's when I realized she had DISAPPEARED.

CHAPTER ELEVEN

When good sheep go BAAd

"Where is she?" I yelled. "What if the vampire sheep have got her?!"

"She can't have gone far," said Fred as we started searching behind some of the gravestones. "She was here a minute ago."

"LILY!" I shouted as loudly as I could. "LILY!"

"Look!" said Fred, pointing to a trail of sticky pink sherbet leading to the other side of the graveyard. "Lily was eating a sherbet dip! She must have gone this way."

"You're right!"

So me and Fred followed the trail until we got to a gate leading out of the graveyard and into a small wood.

"She must be in there!" said Fred.

"LILY, ARE YOU OK?" I shouted into the woods.

"Maggie! I found some lickle lambies! Come see," Lily replied from somewhere among the trees.

Lambs? Oh no...

"Come play with my new pets, Fred and Maggie," said Lily.

"Get away from the lambs, Lily!" I shouted, running into the woods and holding up my

Super Soaker. Fred followed, pulling a spatula from his combat trousers. We ran through the gate and kept going until we came to a clearing where Lily was crouching on the grass just a metre away from two tiny lambs.

"Here, lamby lambykins!" She beckoned to them. "Come to Lily!"

Now I LOVE lambs as much as anyone but NOT these lambs! Because these lambs had actual **EVIL RED EYES AND YELLOW FANGS!** They were vampire lambs aka lampires! But Lily didn't seem to notice. She just stared at them lovingly as if they were fuzzy and cute.

"Lily, we need to go NOW!" I said.

"But I wanna play with the lambies," she said.

"They're not lambs, they're lampires!" I said. "Look at their teeth!"

To my horror, the lambs started to walk closer to Lily, baring their sharp fangs.

"Come on, Lily," Fred yelled, stepping towards her, holding up his spatula. "Let's get out of here!"

"You get Lily and I'll cover you," I told Fred as I pumped up my Super Soaker. "GO!"

Fred managed to get the lambs to back off in alarm by waving his spatula at them, and then he grabbed Lily's hand. He pulled her across the dark woods and back towards the churchyard while I squirted those mini-beasts with my water gun!

However, you might not be very surprised to find out that evil lampires don't care about getting super-soaked one little bit. They just shook the water from their woolly coats and glared at me. Then they "**BAA**-ed" loudly and three bigger sheep stepped out of the trees!

As they all headed towards me, I noticed their eyes seemed even redder, their fangs even sharper, and they looked very, very angry! I had to get out of there. I turned and ran for the gate that led to the churchyard as quickly as I could.

Now you might be thinking that things couldn't *possibly* get any scarier, BUT the thing about stories with vampire sheep in them is this: they always do.

Because I only went and ran smack bang into **BAA**face aka the TERRIFYING vampire sheep leader! He was blocking the gate to the graveyard. And with the other lampires behind me staring out from the woods, I was well and truly trapped!

"You are becoming a real flea in my fleece, kiddo, you know that?" said **BAA**face, headbutting the Super Soaker right out of my hands. "And you wanna know what I do with fleas?"

"Er ... take them for a nice ice cream?" I replied hopefully. "Run them a nice bath?"

"Nah, me and my pals eat them for breakfast!" He laughed evilly. "BAA-Da-Bing."

Then he did a loud "BAA" and suddenly two more vampire sheep joined the lampires in the trees behind me. I was completely surrounded.

Yep. Things had definitely got much, much scarier.

CHAPTER TWELVE

I have run out of BAA jokes, but this chapter is too scary for jokes anyway

Most *ordinary* children would have FAINTED with FEAR if they found themselves stuck in the woods with a gang of bloodthirsty vampire sheep. Well, luckily I am not ordinary children, so I did something else instead. I climbed up a tree and SCREAMED my head off.

"HELP!!!" I yelled. "FRED! MUMMY! ANYONE! HELP!!"

"What's all this noising about, duckaluck? You're giving me the ear jitters!" said a familiar voice, and that's when the tricky old lady appeared from somewhere deep in the woods with her huge handbag! She stood right behind the lampires with her hands on her hips.

"V-v-vampire sh-sh-sheep!" I stuttered.

Now most *normal* little old ladies would be *terrified* if they came face to face with a small flock of vampire sheep in a dark wood. But as I had already discovered, this was no ordinary little old lady. This little old lady did not look scared at all. In fact, she looked very hacked off.

"Oh dear, oh dear, oh dear," she said, rolling up the sleeves of her cardigan. "You have been ~~BAA BAA~~ bad sheep."

You will NOT believe what she did next. She reached into her handbag, pulled out a big flask and unscrewed the lid! We were about to get EATEN by bloodsucking sheep and she was going to pour herself a cup of tea?

"THIS IS NO TIME FOR TEA!" I shouted

down to her in a panic as the sheep totally ignored her and crowded around the bottom of my tree. I clung on to the trunk for dear life.

"This ain't no tea, me duckaluck," she said – and she *threw* the contents of her flask all over the lampires!

Then something really freaky happened. When the "tea", which smelled like garlic and **nightmares** by the way, hit the sheep, their wool started to fizz and a stinky yellow steam came from them. Then their fangs started to get smaller and smaller until they turned back into ordinary sheepy-looking teeth. Then their creepy red eyes faded into ordinary sheepy-looking eyes and then *finally* they all turned back into ordinary sheepy-looking sheep.

The other vampire sheep looked on in horror before turning and running back into the woods. Unfortunately, when the old lady turned to unleash more of her smelly tea on ~~BAA~~face, he had gone!

"Now gets out of here before they come back, duckaluck," the old lady said as she slipped her flask back into her bag and popped a big green lollipop into her mouth.

Shaking, I climbed down from the tree and picked up my Super Soaker. I fumbled to get the gate open and then sped back into the graveyard.

"Thank you for saving me from the dirty rotten vampire sheeps," mumbled the little old lady, following me through the gate. "Oh, don't mention it."

"Oh – um, thank you," I said, still in SHOCK.

"I should think so! Now take these," she said, slipping three snot-coloured lollies into my coat pocket. This lady was OBSESSED with blimming lollipops. "And if I were you, I'd gets out of Knobbly Bottom as soon as you can. It's no place for children."

As the old lady headed back to the fete, I spotted Fred, Lily and my mum running towards me.

"We went to get help!" said Lily, giving me a hug.

"Are you OK?" said my mum. "Fred and Lily said you were scared of some sheep or something?"

"V-vampire sh-sheep and I w-wasn't scared..." I mumbled, suddenly feeling a bit faint. Then I felt all hot and bothered, and my head started to spin with all the stuff that had happened. And before I knew it, I had tumbled to the ground.

CHAPTER THIRTEEN

Another one of my mum's "fun" ideas

When my mum saw me lying on the grass at the fete, she thought I had fainted because I hadn't drunk enough water. Drinking water is *another* thing my mum is OBSESSED with, by the way. She can't leave the house without taking a big bottle of the stuff – anyone would think we were off to the Sahara Desert and not just the park at the end of our street.

Anyway, she took me and Lily straight home and tucked me up in bed with some hot milk and a biscuit! So I didn't get a chance to tell Fred or Lily what had happened to me in the woods.

I decided not to bother telling Mum about the vampire sheep and the little old lady with her flask of smelly garlic tea. She would have just fobbed me off with a **Perfectly Logical Explanation**. Also, she felt so BAD about forgetting to give me some water that she unbanned me from biscuits, and I did NOT want her to change her mind.

Anyway, we were probably safe again now because I BET that brave old lady found the rest of the vampire sheep and soaked them all with her special tea.

SPOILER ALERT. We were not safe. After all, this is a book about SCARY BEASTS...

On Monday morning, I woke up feeling DOUBLE HAPPY because not only were the

vampire sheep (most probably) gone, but I was allowed biscuits again, and I knew for a fact that Mum had a packet of Jammie Dodgers in the cupboard!

But THEN I opened my bedroom curtains and felt DOUBLE UNHAPPY because you'll never guess what I saw? VAMPIRE SHEEP in the field at the end of our garden! There were even more of them than there had been in the barn OR in the woods.

It was such a strange sight. A load of vampire sheep were lined up on the grass with that wily old woolbag BAAface in the middle! And as IF that wasn't scary enough, they all seemed to be staring right up at me

with their creepy red eyes as if to say: "WE ARE COMING FOR YOU!"

I had to find my mum immediately! If she saw THIS creepy crowd, she would definitely move us back to Leicester THAT very day. There was NO WAY she would stay in a village with a massive flock of vampire sheep on the loose!

But guess what? When I ran downstairs and told her there was an enormous gang of evil vampire sheep COMING FOR US and so she HAD to come outside right now, she said she needed to finish the washing-up first! Honestly, grown-ups are so weird. How would clean dishes help us against an army of vampire sheep?

Then she started making jokes like, "Oh, don't you mean a ~~BAA~~rmy of sheep!" and "Is Count Draculamb with them?"

Honestly, mums don't take anything IMPORTANT seriously. So by the time she had washed up and chuckled her way into the garden to see "BAArmageddon" the vampire sheep were completely and utterly gone. Again!

As soon as I had eaten breakfast, I went straight next door and called for Fred. We sat on his front lawn and I told him all about how the tricky old lady had banished some vampire sheep with her flask juice but now there were even MORE out there looking bigger and badder than ever.

"They must have turned more normal sheep into vampires!" said Fred. "There are three farms in this village – if they manage to get to them all we'll be in big trouble!"

"They'll definitely take over the world with that many of them!" I said. "I bet they'll force us to live in barns and give us nothing to eat except grass! We really need the army now, before things get any worse! Can you ask your dad again?"

"But we *still* don't have any proof!" he said.

"What about the photos you took of the vampire sheep?"

Then Fred told me that he had uploaded the photographs to his computer last night, but there must have been something wrong with the camera because there wasn't a single sheep in any of the pictures.

"The field was completely empty apart from what looked like a giant pink finger!" explained Fred.

Then I told him about my mum's phone just videoing my chin, and we decided the vampire sheep must have used their bad magic on Fred's granddad's camera too! We would just have to find another way to get proof.

"But what are we going to do until then?" I said to Fred. "The whole village could be in danger!"

We decided that the first thing we needed to do was to try to find out everything we could about vampire sheep using Fred's phone. His dad got him one so they could stay in touch when he was away. This is *exactly* why I needed a phone. You just never know when you might have a vampire sheep situation to deal with. But do you think my mum cared about that? No, she did not! She just said I have to wait until I'm older, vampire sheep situation or not. But that was another LIE because I asked if I could have a phone tomorrow because I'd be a whole day older then, and she still said NO.

Anyway, here's what we found out about vampire sheep from the internet:

Yep. That's right – a big fat **NOTHING**.

No YouTube videos, no photos, no websites, NOT A SINGLE WOOLLY SAUSAGE. It was almost like nobody in the whole world had ever seen a vampire sheep before ever.

We found a lot of stuff about normal vampires, though. Apparently, you can only get rid of them with garlic, holy water, fire or steaks? They must be allergic to them or something. Was it the same for vampire sheep? We needed to stop those crafty cotton-wool balls on legs before it was too late.

"Well, this is a start!" said Fred.

Just then, my mum came outside to ask if me and Fred wanted to help her and Lily with something "fun".

"Oh yes, please!" said Fred, innocently thinking my mum ACTUALLY meant something FUN. Luckily, I knew better.

"Will there be ice cream, sweets, toys, puppies or roller coasters?" I asked her suspiciously.

"Well, not exactly, but…"

"Cake, bunny rabbits or slime?"

"No. But … how would you like to help me clear out the shed?" she announced. "It's full of old boxes the people who lived here before us must have left behind."

"Well, maybe *they* should come and help you clear it out then," I said.

"That's the strange thing. The landlord said they just disappeared in the middle of the night!" said my mum. "They left no forwarding address or anything! Anyway, come on. I need it clear so I can put your bikes away!"

"No can do I'm afraid, Mother, because we are in the middle of an important mission," I said.

"But this could be an important mission! You might find some hidden treasure in there!" my mum said excitedly.

"More like spiders and mice and shed ghosts!" I sighed.

Then she said she would make us strawberry milkshakes if we helped her, and before I could say "only if we can have squirty cream on them", Fred had already followed her through the gate into our back garden.

When we opened the door to the shed, we saw about six dusty old boxes filled with everything from empty jam jars and gardening tools to half-used paint pots and grubby old rags. There was not going to be ANY hidden treasure in here and my mum knew it!

Then she gave us some bin bags and told us to throw away any old junk but put anything "worth keeping" in a box on the patio and THEN we would get a strawberry milkshake with squirty cream on top. So I started sorting through the boxes with Fred.

You won't be surprised to know that even though we had looked through FOUR boxes and filled two bin bags full of rubbish, we still hadn't found any hidden treasure. Just a LOT of old crockery, rusty tools and three flat footballs. BORING.

Then Lily came out to join us in the shed and asked if we wanted to play snake catchers with the massive PYTHON that was curled up right behind us!

But before you flush this book down the toilet because

snakes are a scary STEP
TOO FAR, then I should tell you
this: when we turned around, we saw
that Lily was looking at a long
green hosepipe and NOT at a
python.

While Lily caught the
hosepipe snake and took it out
into the garden, me and Fred finally opened the
very last box.

And *that* is when we found out...

THE SECRET OF Knobbly Bottom.

CHAPTER FOURTEEN

The secret of Knobbly Bottom

OK, when we first saw what was inside the last dusty old box, we didn't think it was very exciting. It was just full of old newspaper cuttings. (Newspapers are how people got the news before the internet.) In fact, I was about to dump the whole lot straight into the recycling bin when I noticed the headline on one of the cuttings.

I pulled it from the box carefully. The page was so OLD it was all yellow and crispy.

WARNING: Do not turn this page if you are scared of evil beasts, farm animals or evil beasts made out of farm animals.

LOCAL WOMAN SAVES VILLAGE FROM KILLER COWS

A LOCAL woman is believed to have saved an entire village from a herd of killer cows in the early hours of this morning.

Brave Ms Nan Helsing managed to lure the bloodthirsty beasts, whose eyes were described by witnesses as "red and glowing", away from the terrified villagers of Knobbly Bottom and into an unused barn.

Helsing emerged from the barn several minutes later carrying a lollipop, followed by a herd of perfectly ordinary, friendly looking cows. Nan Helsing said of the incident: "No comment, me duckaluck."

OMG! *Killer Cows?* I showed Fred and we started pulling out more cuttings. It seemed **Knobbly Bottom** was even scarier than we thought!

  THE KNOBBLY NEWS: JULY 13th 1980

BIG FOOT SPOTTED IN VILLAGE

RESIDENTS of Knobbly Bottom claim to have seen a mysterious Big Foot-like figure prowling the village during the night. For the past week, the six-foot creature has been spotted helping himself to chickens from several local farms.

Chicken farmer Tim Slopsy said: "I came outside and saw this humungous creature munching greedily on one of my chickens like he was at KFC or something!"

No photographic evidence of the beast has been captured.

GREEDY PIGS GROW HORNS

VILLAGERS in Knobbly Bottom claim their homes are under attack from unusually greedy pigs.

The local pigs, who eyewitnesses claim have grown horns and sharp teeth overnight, are eating everything in sight.

Pig farmer Roy Saveloy said: "I know pigs eat a lot, but this is ridiculous. They've gobbled up everything in my garden including a swingball set, three footballs and my cat Fluffy."

This must be why the people who left the shed boxes behind moved out so quickly! Maybe weird things happened to *them* in **Knobbly Bottom** and they got scared!

"Look at this, Maggie!" said Fred, picking up the "killer cows" newspaper cutting. "Does this 'Nan Helsing' look familiar to you?"

126

There was a photograph of a tricky-looking lady in front of a herd of cows, sucking on a LOLLIPOP!

"It's the lady who saved me from the sheep! She's younger there, but I'd recognize that tricky face anywhere!" I said, gathering up the cuttings. "I'm going to show my mum these. She will *definitely* move back to Leicester once she knows how scary Knobbly Bottom really is!"

But the thing about taking newspaper cuttings outside when Lily is playing snake catchers is this: you will almost certainly trip over a six-foot hosepipe python and drop EVERYTHING!

Then, before you know it, your PRECIOUS PROOF has blown right over the garden fence and into the field of … CAN YOU GUESS? Yep, that's right. Flipping sheep.

"We need to get those newspaper cuttings back!" I said to Fred, looking over at the sheep who were munching on the green grass. "But how can we when they've gone into the VAMPIRE SHEEP FIELD?"

"Wait. Those look like ordinary sheep to me!" said Fred.

And I couldn't argue with that because, when I looked across the field, these ones *did* actually look like ordinary sheep. No red eyes or sharp teeth or anything! No doubt BAAface and his gang were the other side of **Knobbly Bottom** working on their evil plans.

"We could just jump over the fence, grab the papers and run back!" said Fred. "They probably won't even notice."

So Fred climbed into the field and started

running towards the newspapers, which were fluttering about in the breeze. So far, so good…

But you will NOT believe what happened next! He was *literally* about three steps away from the sheep when they stopped munching on the thick green grass and looked up at him. Then THIS happened!

1. The ordinary sheep's eyes turned RED.

2. The ordinary sheep grew sharp FANGS.

3. The ordinary sheep GROWLED.

4. The ordinary sheep were no longer ordinary sheep. They had turned into…
   VAMPIRE SHEEP.

They snarled at Fred – which is a very ODD thing to see a sheep do – and started marching towards him!

Luckily, Fred is a *really* fast runner, so he abandoned the newspapers, legged it over to the fence and vaulted back into our garden.

"What just happened?!" Fred panted. "They were normal one minute, then … then…"

"They TURNED! Maybe they had already been *bitten*? Did they look bitten?" I said.

But before Fred could answer, you will not believe what those woolly wallies did? Those ROTTEN vampire sheep only went and ATE our PROOF! They gobbled up the newspaper cuttings and then scurried off across the field looking very pleased with themselves.

"This is all your fault, Lily!" I yelled. "I wouldn't have dropped the newspapers if your stupid 'snake' hadn't tripped me over!"

"That's why I'm trying to catch it!" said Lily, picking up the hose and chucking it back into the shed. "Naughty snake."

Then she went inside to tell my mum how she had rescued ME from a snake. UGH!

I rummaged through the box to see if I could find any more EVIDENCE for Mum and the army, but all I found were some old electricity bills and pizza menus.

So then Fred said we should ask his granddad if he has any more "intel" (apparently that is army speak for information), because he has lived in **Knobbly Bottom** for years and knows everybody and everything. Maybe he would know more about the vampire sheep?

We told my mum we would have our milkshakes later, and then we ran next door to find Mr Tibble and told him *everything*.

"Vampire sheep, you say?" He gestured at us to sit at the kitchen table. "What a thing! Well, don't worry, me dears. I know exactly what we need to do."

Finally, a grown-up who believes us, I thought.

He will probably call the army himself and get them to Knobbly Bottom TODAY!

"What we need to do is ... have ourselves a nice cuppa tea!" said Mr Tibble, boiling the kettle.

One thing you should know about Mr Tibble is that he is OBSESSED with cups of tea. Which is fine if you like tea, but NOT very helpful if you are trying to stop a PACK OF VAMPIRE SHEEP from taking over a village.

"But Granddad!" said Fred. "What about the sheep?"

"I don't think sheep like tea," he said. "Now would you like milk and sugar, me dears?"

This was not going well.

"Mr Tibble, do you know a lady called Nan Helsing?" I asked.

"Oooh, the delightful Nan Helsing!" said Mr Tibble, smiling. "I've always had a bit of a soft spot for her, ya know. Lovely smile and huge muscles."

"Does she live in Knobbly Bottom?" said Fred.

"Yep! Lives in an old farmhouse on top of Knobs Hill! But she's usually off gallivanting somewhere or other in her camper van!" he said. "She's off to Spain today, I think. Said she needed a bit of sunshine."

This was NOT good news! The only person who could help us defeat the evil vampire sheep was leaving the country! Fred looked as worried as I felt.

"Biscuits, me dears?" said Mr Tibble, opening a packet of chocolate digestives as if this would solve the problem.

Fred shrugged at me as he watched his granddad pour water into an enormous teapot.

And that was that! We had NO proof and not one single grown-up was going to help us stop the vampire sheep. Fred even tried texting his dad in capital letters to show that he MEANT BUSINESS:

VAMPIRE SHEEP TAKING OVER THE VILLAGE. SEND HELP AND ARMY TANKS NOW.

But his dad just replied saying:

Sounds like a fun game, son!

Parents are so annoying.

Then we tried telling my mum about the newspaper cuttings, but she just said they were probably FAKE newspapers that somebody had made up for a joke!

There must be someone else in the village who KNEW something!

"What about the shopkeeper?" suggested Fred. "He might have some intel!"

"The Great and Evil Child-Eater?" I said. "I'd rather take my chances with the vampire sheep!"

In the end we decided there was only one thing for it. We would just have to save the world from the vampire sheep **all by ourselves.**

But we needed to do it soon because once that beastly ~~BAA~~face and his gang had turned every sheep in the village into vampires, we'd NEVER be able to stop them.

CHAPTER FIFTEEN

A LOT at "steak"

At this point in the story, you are probably thinking that we were DOOMED because...

1. An entire army of vampire sheep was about to take over the WORLD and make us live in the fields and eat grass!
2. The only person who knew how to stop them was on her way to Spain.

BUT you do NOT have to worry because we were NOT doomed. Why? Because there was someone super brave and super good at hide-and-seek who was going to STOP those rotten sheep and save the day. Not Batman, not Wonder

Woman, not even Taylor Swift with a big sword, but ME, Maggie McKay.

"But how?" asked Fred when I told him this. "You're just a nine-year-old girl, Maggie, and, no offence, a bit on the small side. I bet you haven't even got any Save the World from Sheep weapons!"

So then *I* said that Harry Potter was just an *ordinary* boy who lived in a flipping cupboard and *he* managed to save an entire school from evil magic without even losing his glasses.

"He was also a wizard, Maggie!" Fred pointed out.

"OK, well, what about that *ordinary* girl on the news who is always saving the world from the environment?" I said. "The way I see it, there's absolutely no reason with a cherry on top why I can't be a hero too!"

"Good point. BUT you are going to need help. *Maybe* from someone with army training, binoculars and one of these bad boys," said Fred, pulling a huge frying pan out of his belt and waving it around proudly. "It's a Frytastic 2000, aluminium and non-stick! Great for bacon and bashing stuff."

What was it with Fred and kitchen utensils?

"OK, OK, I get the point!" I said. "You and your big pan can help me banish the vampire sheep."

"Wondergirl help too!" yelled Lily, running over to us with a tea towel cape tied around her neck and a stick in her hand. "Da-da-daaaaaah!" She did her best superhero pose and waved her stick at us. "I'll get the bad guys!"

"But *how* do we do it?" asked Fred, tucking his pan back into his belt. "We couldn't find anything on the internet about getting rid of vampire sheep!"

"Steak!" I said.

"This is no time to be thinking about dinner, Maggie!" said Fred. "Although I could actually whip you up a tasty steak with my Frytastic!"

"Not for me, for the sheep!" I said.

"I don't think cooking the vampire sheep a nice meal is going to stop them!" said Fred. "They're evil, remember?"

"No! Remember on the internet it said how normal vampires can be banished with steaks? Well, guess what? There is a whole packet of beefburgers in our freezer, which are made from steak!"

"Oh yes! And my granddad has a few rump steaks in the fridge too!" said Fred.

So we came up with another brilliant plan! This one was so dangerous that it would definitely get me banned from biscuits for LIFE if my mum found out. But that didn't matter because when I saved the world from vampire sheep, the prime minister would probably give me ten million biscuits as a reward.

In just a few easy steps we would banish those vampire sheep for ever!

MAGGIE, FRED AND ~~LILY'S~~ WONDERGIRL'S PLAN

Step 1: Get steak and burgers from freezers and hide them in Maggie's Hello Kitty rucksack

~~Step 2: Make catapults~~

Step 2: Find out how to make catapults from YouTube

Step 3: Make catapults

Step 4: Find the vampire sheep

Step 5: Catapult steak at the vampire sheep

Step 6: Receive Saving the World award and biscuits from prime minister

*

If I told my mum about **The Plan** I KNEW she would NOT let me do it. She won't even let me go to the park on my own, so she definitely wouldn't let me go and hurl steak at some vampire sheep on my own. She probably wouldn't believe me anyway and would say it was a waste of burgers. That was why me and Fred had NO choice but to SNEAK OUT AT NIGHT and do it when the grown-ups were asleep.

"But why can't I come, Maggie?" said Lily when we told her that **Operation Steak the Sheep** was too dangerous for a five-year-old. "Superheroes are not scared of sheep!"

"That's why we need you to stay home!" I said. "Someone needs to protect Mummy from the vampire sheep!"

Lily seemed to be happy with that. Well, she did after I gave her half of the secret stash of jelly babies I kept in a shoebox under my bed. Rav says you should always keep sweets under your bed for emergency bribes, and he was right.

I know you are probably thinking: *"Don't do it, Maggie! Nothing good ever comes from sneaking out at midnight with a Hello Kitty rucksack full of beef!"*

Well, I HATE to tell you that you are right. Nothing good did come of it because later that night we discovered we had made a BIG mistake. Can you guess what it was?

CHAPTER SIXTEEN

Our big mis-steak

The Plan started really well. I had a rucksack FULL of burgers and steak! We had managed to sneak out without my mum *or* Mr Tibble catching us, and we were heading across the field at the end of my garden, catapults at the ready!

The only problem was, when we got to the field it was completely deserted!

"The barn!" I said. "Where ~~BAA~~face held the evil plan meeting – I bet that's their headquarters!"

So Fred and I trudged across the cold, dark field until we came to the big old barn. We tiptoed up to the door and heard lots of

~~BAA~~-ing, laughing and loud gangster-type voices coming from inside. It was them!

"Right, catapults at the ready!" I whispered, and we got our chunks of steak ready to launch! "Burgers loaded!" said Fred, putting half a burger in a catapult.

"Then let's go sling some steak!" I said and kicked the barn door open – which would have looked very cool indeed if it had not been LOCKED.

"OW!" I gasped, hopping about on the foot that hadn't been bashed by a barn door.

Just then the door flew open from the inside. As ~~BAA~~face and the vampire sheep piled out of the barn, looking very annoyed, Fred and I dived behind a bale of hay before he could spot us. We held up our meat-filled catapults…

"READY?" I whispered to Fred. He nodded, and we climbed on top of the hay bale. "AIM. FIRE!"

Then we slung burger chunk after burger chunk at the puzzled-looking sheep until everything went completely silent and we slunk back down behind the hay bale, exhausted.

"Did it work?" whispered Fred.

I shrugged and slowly peeped over the hay. But the vampire sheep were still there and looking as healthy and evil as ever! Maybe the steak took a few minutes to kick in – I hoped.

But then the beastly brutes looked at the chunks of beef on the floor around them and started to LAUGH!

~~BAA~~face sniffed a huge chunk of steak that had landed by his feet.

"Oh, rump steak! My favourite," he said. And then he started wolfing down Mr Tibble's steak AND my burgers so quickly he did a massive stinky steak burp. The other sheep joined in and soon those greedy beasts had polished off every last bit of the meat we had slung at them. And they were STILL flipping vampires!

"The internet is such a liar!" I said to Fred. "It definitely said you can get rid of vampires with steak."

~~BAA~~face and the sheep started laughing again.

"Wrong kinda steak, kids! Now, get 'em, gang!" said ~~BAA~~face.

This was it! We were done for! The sheep all started moving towards us like a big, evil cloud. I could almost smell their meaty, burpy breath on my face, but then they saw something walking across the field that made them stop and stare!

There was a PANDA BEAR coming towards us in the darkness! This village was getting weirder by the minute. And just when we thought things couldn't get any stranger than a gang of steak-gobbling vampire sheep versus a panda bear, we noticed that the panda was carrying a Super Soaker.

As it got even closer we saw it was ... LILY! In her panda dressing gown! She must have followed us out of the house!

"Lily!" I yelled and beckoned for her to join us behind the hay bale. "I told you to stay home! The steak didn't work. We're done for!"

"I couldn't get to sleep. I tried counting sheep but that made me think about the scary ones and then I was wide awake!" Lily said as we heard the sheep muttering about what to do with pesky panda bears and crafty kids. "Are they going to eat us up?"

"I won't let them. I just need to think of a way out of here!" I said, peeping over the hay. BAAface was approaching – just a few steps away from us now.

"Get lost, woolface!" Fred shouted. "I've had army training and I'm not afraid to use it!"

"Thanks for the steak, kiddos!" growled BAAface. "Now it's time for dessert!"

The vampire sheep edged closer, with their fanged mouths wide open, until we were totally surrounded.

But luckily I got another BRILLIANT idea, and it was all thanks to Lily. These rotten woolbags might be evil vampires but they were still SHEEP.

I took a deep breath and climbed on top of the hay bale so I was almost eye to eye with BAAface. He was now standing on his hind legs and looking terrifyingly tall.

"Wait a minute, Mister BAAface!" I said in my best brave-hero voice. "I actually have some more juicy steak in my bag! It'll be a much tastier dessert than us. I haven't had a bath for three days!"

BAAface paused. "Well, it *was* real good steak. We could finish that off *before* we get to dessert. Whaddya say, gang?" he asked his hungry-looking crew. They nodded greedily.

"But, er, first, how many of you are there? I want to check I have enough to give you all an equal portion? Unless, of course, sheep can't count!" I said.

"How dare you? BAAface ain't no dummy!" he said, and he started to count his gang.

"One, two, three…"

This had to work. It was our only chance to escape.

"What are you doing?" hissed Fred.

"You'll see!" I whispered back, crossing my fingers.

"Four, five, six, seven…" BAAface yawned.

Then … guess WHAT? BAAface seemed to get sleepier and sleepier with every sheep he counted, and by the time he got to number twenty-one, he was snoring on the cold, wet grass like a big baby. Not only that, but he appeared to have sent the other vampire sheep to sleep too!

"It worked!" I said. "Counting sheep sends you to sleep, even when you are one!"

"Genius!" said Fred.

And it hadn't just worked on the sheep. Poor Lily was fast asleep too, curled up on the hay.

"Don't worry!" said Fred. "My dad says one of the first things they teach you in army training is how to give piggybacks!"

We carefully lifted a yawning Lily on to Fred's back just as the sheep were starting to stir! "They're waking up!" I said. "RUN!"

So we SPRINTED across the field and over the fence into the safety of my back garden.

That was when I decided I would NEVER sling-shot steaks at vampire sheep EVER again.

And even though we'd got away this time, I was starting to think we'd never defeat this fearsome flock. They were too strong and there were too many of them.

Maybe we were doomed after all.

CHAPTER SEVENTEEN

Yet another brilliant plan goes wrong

You've probably already guessed the BIG mistake we made in the last chapter. Apparently, you use STAKES (aka wooden pointy things) to defeat vampires and not STEAK (aka blunt beefy things).

It ended up being the worst plan EVER for two reasons:

1. It didn't work because we got the wrong kind of steak; and

2. I forgot to empty my Hello Kitty rucksack and Mum found a mouldy raw burger in there three days later.

STEAK

STAKE

She was NOT happy. Obviously I couldn't tell her WHY there was a soggy raw burger in my rucksack or I would have got in BIG trouble for sneaking out and going sheep-steaking, so I told her it was for my pet rat.

"But you don't have a pet rat," she said.

Then I said that was exactly why it was still in my bag and not inside a rat's tummy, so if she thought about it, it was all HER fault.

Anyway, back to the **VAMPIRES.** We needed another plan super FAST! Luckily, I am an expert at plans, so I soon came up with a brilliant idea that had absolutely nothing to do with raw meat.

On Tuesday, it was really, really hot in **Knobbly Bottom**. The sun was shining and there were no clouds in the sky. In fact, it was so hot that none of the growns-ups seemed to believe it.

"I can't believe how hot it is today," said my mum, opening the curtains. She even rang my nana JUST to ask whether she could believe how hot it was! Then I heard Mr Tibble telling the postman that HE couldn't believe how warm the weather was and GUESS WHAT? The postman said he couldn't either. Maybe in the olden days they didn't learn about the seasons at school and that's why grown-ups get confused when it is hot in the actual summer.

Anyway, because of this "unbelievably" hot weather, my mum said we could invite Fred over and have a water fight in the garden! So that afternoon, Fred, Lily and me were having a water fight with our Super Soakers, and that was when I came up with my non-steak-throwing plan.

"We could use our Super Soakers to defeat the vampire sheep!" I said excitedly, waving my Turbo 300 around.

"I don't think you can stop bloodthirsty vampires with water pistols, Maggie!" said

Fred. "And didn't you already try squirting them with water at the fete and they just shook it off?"

"Yes, but that was just normal water from the tap!" I said. "We won't be squirting them with normal water from the tap. We will use special anti-vampire juice!"

"Where do we get that from?" asked Lily.

"Well, everyone knows that vampires are allergic to garlic," I said. "So we mix garlic into the water and soak them with that!"

"I bet that's what Nan Helsing had in her flask!" said Fred. "We're going to need plenty of it now there are loads of vampire sheep."

"That's OK. We can fill up water balloons and bottles too! And put some in big buckets for when we need to reload!" I said.

"There's just one problem," said Fred. "How do we get all the buckets, bottles and Super Soakers to the vampire sheep?"

"We don't! We get them to come to us!"

Then I told him the absolute cleverest part of my plan.

"We know they are looking for more sheep to turn into vampires, right?" I said, running inside to get some paper and pens. Then I made this sign.

LAMBS LAMBS LAMBS! DO YOU LOVE LAMBS?

Then why not come along to

the Pop-Up Lamb Petting Zoo!

Lots of lovely lambs that definitely

aren't vampires yet, here waiting for you!

Free steak on arrival.

ALL WELCOME! WEDNESDAY 10 A.M.

Back Garden, 3 The Green, Knobbly Bottom

"Perfect. They won't be able to resist the chance to make more 'lampires'!" said Fred. "But wait, how do we know vampire sheep can read?"

"I saw them! They were reading a map in the barn," I replied. "Now we just need to put these signs all around the village so the sheep will see them!"

"OK, I'll put them up when me and my granddad walk the dog later!" said Fred.

"Brilliant! This time tomorrow those filthy furballs will be back to being brilliantly boring sheep!" I smiled. "And we'll be heroes!"

CHAPTER EIGHTEEN

The problem with trying to save the world in your back garden

The problem with having a plan to save the world that take place in your own back garden is this: your mum might decide to hang out some washing!

We were all ready to go. We had opened the gate at the end of the garden so the sheep could get in. We had Super Soakers, bottles and buckets full of anti-vampire juice.

HOW TO MAKE ANTI-VAMPIRE JUICE

1. Get as much garlic as you can from your kitchen cupboards.

2. Raid your piggy bank and ask a kindly neighbour who won't ask too many questions (Mr Tibble) to buy you ten garlic bulbs from the shop.

3. Borrow your mum's smoothie maker and make the bulbs into a smooth paste at your garlic crushing station (Fred's kitchen). FYI, this will make your mum's breakfast smoothies taste weirdly garlicky for weeks afterwards, so if she offers you one do **NOT** accept.

4. Mix the garlic paste with water (one big spoonful per empty lemonade bottle of water) with a wooden stake (sharp twig from the garden).

Lily was crouching behind the apple tree with a bag full of Vampire Blaster Bombs (water balloons full of the garlicky water), and we had put a big sign on the fence saying *LAMB PETTING ZOO*.

Fred was hiding behind the shed with his water pistol and big frying pan, and I was standing guard by the back door in case my mum tried to come out and do something really annoying like HANG OUT THE SILLY OLD WASHING. If the vampire sheep saw my mum doing laundry they would NOT believe it was a real lamb petting zoo! Plus, she would ask us what the heck we were doing with a load of garlic-flavoured water.

Luckily, I had an idea. Right as my mum came towards the back door, I asked her if I could have some fruit. BUT I knew for a fact that the only fruit we had was melon and mango, aka stuff you needed to cut up with the sharp knife that I wasn't allowed to use! My mum is *always* trying to get me to "eat more fruit and vegetables" so I knew she would JUMP at the chance and go and make me a Healthy Snack!

I am a genius, I thought to myself.

At least, I thought I was a genius until it all went wrong.

As soon as my mum went back into the house, I ducked behind the shed with Fred, and we waited there as quiet as mice, our anti-vampire-juice-filled Super Soakers at the ready!

A few seconds later a couple of nasty-looking sheep slipped into the garden, sniffing around the grass in search of fresh lambs for their vampire collection!

They looked much bigger and meaner than I remembered. Their eyes were redder and their fangs were sharper. In other words, they looked REALLY REEEALLLY SCARY.

Some of them were bigger than Lily! And the problem with vampire sheep who are bigger than Lily is this: if you were an actual Lily-sized

Lily, it was absolutely terrifying. Especially as they were heading right towards her!

So I wasn't too surprised when, instead of pelting them with her garlicky water balloons LIKE WE HAD PLANNED, she went into shock and FROZE.

Then, just when we thought things couldn't get any worse, two MORE huge vampire sheep came bustling through the back gate towards poor Lily!

"Over here, you rotten balls of wool!" shouted Fred, leaping out from our hiding place. "There are lots of juicy lambs inside this shed!"

Then those greedy vampire sheep growled and trotted towards him! Fred pointed his Super Soaker at them while I ran over and grabbed Lily's hand. She was still frozen with SHOCK as about a DOZEN more vampire sheep piled through the gate.

"Come on, Lily!" I yelled, trying to pull her

towards the back door.

"WE WANT LAMBS!" bleated one dirty-looking sheep standing right in front of us. "WHERE ARE THE LAMBS?"

"Ermmm. Behind you!" I shouted and

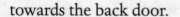

pointed behind the baffled-looking beast. The vampire sheep turned round and that was when I took my chance! I squirted it three times AND hurled a couple of water balloons at its woolly butt for good measure!

At first, nothing happened.

The vampire sheep just shook the drips from its woolly coat and glared up at me with big red eyes. Suddenly I felt like our plan was DOOMED.

But then something really grosstastic happened... The wool that was damp with my anti-vampire juice fizzed slightly and let off a sort of stinky steam like a gone-off kettle boiling. The sheep's eyes seemed to switch between red and brown, as if they couldn't decide what colour they were, and he hung his head as if suddenly confused. Then he stumbled backwards and lay down on the lawn! The anti-vampire juice must have weakened him because he fell asleep on the grass right in front of us! The strange thing was that he didn't fizzle and turn back into a normal sheep like the ones in the woods had after being soaked in Nan's brew. Maybe our recipe wasn't strong enough so it might take a bit longer to work?

But before I could enjoy my small victory, another vampire sheep BAA-ed at me.

"WHERE ARE THE LAMBS?" it croaked.

By now, our garden was FULL of those filthy beasts of all different shapes and sizes. But our plan was working! Fred had climbed up on to the shed roof and was super-soaking as many of them as he could. Great big squirts of garlic water were flying across the garden and sizzling sheep left, right and centre.

Luckily, Lily had UNFROZEN and was now chucking her water bombs at as many sheep as she could too. (Unfortunately, because Lily wasn't very good at throwing, she mostly got my leg, the gate and the apple tree.)

Meanwhile, I squirted my Super Soaker at every vicious vamp that came near us.

Then those rancid ratbags started shouting things so TERRIBLE that you might have to go and eat three chocolate biscuits just to get the taste out of your head.

"Give us lambs, you two-legged losers," said a particularly gruesome-looking vampire sheep, coming towards me and Lily, baring his teeth. "Or prepare to be herded into hell!"

"Lambs, lambs, lambs!" they shouted furiously.

They had us surrounded. For every sheep we managed to send into a snooze with our anti-vampire juice, another two seemed to come wandering into the garden! We wouldn't be able to hold them off for much longer...

I looked over at Fred on the shed roof. His Super Soaker had run out of juice, and a couple of the vampire sheep were trying to climb on top of each other's backs to reach him! Luckily, he managed to shoo them away with his pan, but they kept coming!

"My Super Soaker is empty now too!" I yelled to Fred over the loud ~~BAA~~-ing of the vampire sheep.

I checked my pocket for more water bombs, but all I found was a few sticky, smelly old lollipops. That's when I realized they were the ones Nan Helsing had given me at the fete! They had an odd smell to them. I held the green lollies to my nose and sniffed.

"Garlic-flavoured lollies!" I shouted up to Fred. "Nan Helsing must have been trying to protect us!"

I popped one in my mouth, gave one to Lily, and it's lucky I'm so good at throwing stuff because I managed to lob one right up to Fred on the shed roof! We sucked the lollies as hard as we could and then blew our stinky breath all over those pesky beasts that were just steps away from us! And even though the lollies were GROSS, we didn't mind because one sniff of us and the sheep backed away!

"I'll hold them off while you get Lily inside!" shouted Fred from the shed roof, aiming a few garlicky burps at the sheep below him.

"OK, I'll try to find more garlic and meet you back out here!" I said, grabbing Lily's hand. We leapt over some sleepy sheep as we sprinted for the back door.

We ran into the kitchen – only to come face to face with my mum.

"How many times do I have to tell you NOT to slam the door?" said Mum, who was carrying a big bowl full of sliced melon and mango.

"Sorry, but we are in the middle of trying to escape from the ARMY OF VAMPIRE SHEEP that FYI are in our back garden!" I said.

"Oh, Maggie! Not more of your stories. You're scaring your poor sister," she said, looking at Lily, who was as white as a ghost. "For the last time, there are no such things as monsters!"

But one second later, she dropped the bowl of fruit to the floor and stared open-mouthed at something behind us. Something big and woolly had just butted open the back door!

A HUGE VAMPIRE SHEEP was now standing in our kitchen!!

CHAPTER NINETEEN

Panic in the pantry

At this point, I would have loved to shout at my mum, "I TOLD YOU THERE ARE SUCH THINGS AS MONSTERS!" but I was too busy freaking out because *another two vampire sheep* were coming inside!

Mum suddenly looked very pale, and the next thing I knew she was shoving us all into the pantry and slamming the door behind us.

"What the *heck* is going on?" she asked, back pressed against the pantry door.

"Well, like I have been trying to tell you," I said, "there are beasts in Knobbly Bottom! Beasts like VAMPIRE SHEEP!"

But before I could say anything else, we

heard Fred screaming outside!

I scrambled to the small pantry window just in time to see him being BOUNCED along the garden on the backs of the vampire sheep! They must have managed to knock him off the roof of the shed! It looked like they were trying to BUMP him all the way out of the garden – and he had dropped his garlic lollipop and his Super Soaker.

"We need to get out of here and help Fred!" I yelled, right as we heard more vampire sheep butting their heads against the pantry door.

"But there are big bad sheep out there!" cried Lily.

"**BAA BAAAAAAA**," the vampire sheep bleated from the kitchen. Then there was a sudden loud bang and the wooden pantry door started to splinter away from its hinges. We had to do something before the sheep broke it down!

"Right!" I said in my best superhero voice. "We need more garlic!"

Jumping into action, my mum rifled through the cupboards as quickly as she could.

"Oh no," she said as another bash and a **BAA** came from the other side of the door. "We're all out of garlic!"

"And there are no more lollipops!" said Lily, her eyes opened wide in terror as she watched my mum frantically opening the freezer.

"OK, girls. We might not have any garlic bulbs BUT we do have … garlic bread and a garlicky sausage pizza!" said my mum, whipping out three frozen garlic baguettes and a large sausage supreme and pulling them from their wrappers. "Pooh! One sniff of these bad boys and those vampire sheep will be quaking in their woolly coats!"

"B-but aren't you scared?" said Lily, hugging my mum's legs.

"Of course I am!" said Mum, pulling me and Lily in for a hug.

Then she told us a BIG secret of her own.

First, she said that she is absolutely terrified of WASPS.

"But you can't be!" I said. "You *always* get them when they come in the house! Even the big fat ones!"

"That's because you and Lily are afraid of them," she said. "And luckily when you become a mummy, you get this very cool superpower that makes you brave even when you're really scared."

"Really?" I said.

"Really." Mum smiled. "And I happen to know that big sisters get that very same superpower!"

"But they're big, evil vampire sheep!" I said.

"Yes, but we are THE FANTASTIC THREE!" my mum said as another bang on the door made the wood *crunch*.

"YES!" I cheered and we did our **Fantastic Three** high five, which is basically like a normal high five but we shout "GO, FANTASTIC THREE!" at the end.

Then my mum rolled up her sleeves, put her hair up in one of her Get Stuff Done buns and handed out the garlicky frozen food.

"But it's just garlic bread!" cried Lily.

"This is *not* garlic bread, Lily," my mum said,

waving her baguette in the air like a sword. "It's a Vampire Zapper!"

"Yay!" cheered Lily, swishing the garlic bread above her head.

"Are you 'bready' to go, girls?" Mum said, holding up her baguette and smiling even though this was definitely NOT the time for one of her jokes.

"Yes – let's go save Fred and stop the beasts!" I said.

"Wait!" cried Lily. "I need a … a … p—"

"Oh no!" me and Mum said in horror. *Not now, Lily!*

"A power helmet!" said Lily, grabbing a large plastic mixing bowl and popping it on her head. *Phew!*

"One, two … Fantastic Three to the rescue!" my mum yelled – before KICKING open the door.

CHAPTER TWENTY

The Fantastic Three (and friends) to the rescue

WARNING: this is the SCARIEST chapter of this whole book. So if you don't like scary stuff then I suggest you LOOK AWAY now.

After my mum kicked open the pantry door, we stepped into the kitchen, waving our baguettes at the vampire sheep. And sure enough, as soon as they sniffed those smelly garlic fumes, they went running back out into the garden BAA-ing like scaredy-lambs.

We followed them out, wafting our whiffy weapons in their faces until they slowly but surely started to look a bit less scary and a little more sleepy!

I shouted over to Fred, who had managed to

turn around and sit on a sheep like he was riding a horse, holding on to its grubby coat for dear life!

I frisbeed the sausage supreme right at the gruesome beast, and as the garlicky pizza spun right under its nose, it yawned and lay down. Then Fred jumped off and ran over to join us, so I snapped my garlic baguette in two (which is NOT as easy as it sounds, by the way. I had to whack it on the floor several times before it came apart!) and handed one half to him.

Now don't freak out, BUT at this point there were about fifteen vampire sheep on our lawn! It was a very strange sight. Some were fast asleep from the garlic fumes, some were drowsy, and some, who were yet to be "garlicked", were staring right at us with their sharp fangs out, looking VERY, VERY cross.

"RIGHT!" said my mum, pointing her baguette at the angry creatures. "I want all of you vampire sheep out of my garden, or ELSE!"

Now me and Lily knew full well that when Mum says "or else" it basically just means she will tell us to do the thing again but in a LOUDER voice, but the vampire sheep did NOT know that. In fact, they looked pretty worried!

"Yeah!" I shouted, waving my garlic bread at them menacingly. "So unless you want three bags full of ELSE, you had better go away!"

Then, forming a chain, the four of us wafted our baguettes at the vampire sheep as hard as we could, until one by one they made their way back through the gate and into the field, looking very "sheepish" and ~~BAA~~-ing at us sleepily. Then my mum ran over and slammed the gate behind them.

"Well done, Fantastic Three … and Fred!" Mum cheered, hugging me and Lily tightly as the sleepy sheep wandered off across the field and fell into woozy naps on the grass. "They really are very strange sheep!"

Then Mum said we all deserved some biscuits for being so brave, so she went inside to get a big plate of chocolate Hobnobs!

"We actually did it!" I said to Fred, rubbing my hands together. "When they wake up they'll be totally normal sheep! Mission accomplished!"

"Maggie…" said Fred.

"We'll probably get some kind of bravery medal for this and…"

"But Maggie…" said Fred, a little louder this time.

"Or a Nobel Peace Prize! Do you think the prime minister will want to meet us? I expect we'll be on the television and…"

"MAGGIE, LOOK!" Fred shouted and pointed across the field.

You know in scary films when the goodies think they've won and they're cheering and looking all pleased with themselves? Then SUDDENLY a leftover baddie jumps out on them from behind a tree or something when they least expect it?

Well, that is sort of what happened next. Except much, much **worse.** Because it wasn't just ONE leftover baddie – it was a whole FLOCK of them.

Every single one of the sheep had woken up, BUT they were still vampires! Not only that but about a ZILLION more had come to join them. They were all standing on the horizon like a big woolly sunset!

"Uh-oh!" said Lily.

"Uh-oh with knobs on!" I said.

"We're going to need a LOT more garlic!" said Fred.

Our now-defrosted and super-soggy baguettes would be no match for this huge army.

Then we heard footsteps coming up the garden path from the front gate. This time it wasn't a vampire sheep, but it was…

Gary the Great and Evil Child-Eater!

"A lambing zoo? I knew yous kids would be trouble," he said, waving one of our Lamb Petting Zoo signs at us.

So not only was a vampire sheep army approaching, but we now had great and evil child-eating Gary in our garden! Was he in the vampire sheep gang? Maybe he was a vampire too?

But before any of us could reply to Gary, a loud engine sound came from the field and made us all jump!

And you will never guess who was riding across the field on a giant tractor with an extra-big lollipop in her mouth?

Nan Helsing!

CHAPTER TWENTY-ONE

The mighty Monster Muck Spreader

As Nan Helsing drove towards our garden fence, we noticed hers was NO ordinary tractor. It had a massive funnel on the front that was spraying smelly yellow liquid all over the field. Liquid that smelled like … garlic!

"What on earth is that?" I said.

"That be a muck spreader! The farmers use it to spread manure across their fields," said Mr Tibble, who had come out to see what all the noise was about. "Anyone for a cuppa?"

"What's manure?" asked Lily.

"It's nature's very own fertilizer, my girl!" said Mr Tibble.

"It's poo!" I whispered to a confused-looking Lily.

"YUCK!" Lily said.

"This is my Monster Muck Spreader actually," said Nan, overtaking the vampire sheep and pulling up next to our garden fence. "It be full of a special brew that will get rid of those good-for-nothing beasts!"

"But I thought you were in Spain!" Fred said.

"I was on my way when I saw your Lamb Petting Zoo signs!" said Nan. "I thought you might run into a spot of the troubles!"

"But we tried garlicky water and it didn't get rid of the vampires – it just made them fall asleep for a while!" I shouted at Nan.

"This ain't made with no normal water, though, me duckalucks. This be holy water," said Nan. "Garlic on its own just weakens 'em."

"How do you get holes in water?" asked a confused Lily.

"Not holey, *holy*," said Nan. "From the church.

Vampires are very allergic to it. Freshly blessed by the vicar this morning. Anyway, no time for chittery chattery, the beasts are a-coming!"

The vampire sheep were only a few metres away from our garden fence now! Whatever Nan was going to do, she needed to do it quick! She grabbed two large sacks from inside her muck spreader and threw them down to us.

"Monster missiles," she said, pointing at the bags. "Garlic bulbs soaked in holy water."

Fred and Lily grabbed handfuls of the garlic missiles while Gary picked up Lily's hosepipe snake and attached it to the garden tap.

"We've flooded the Knobbly Bottom water supply with Nan's anti-vampire juice, so you soaks any beasties that comes in the garden!" he said, throwing me the hosepipe before hopping over the fence and on to the muck spreader with Nan.

"And me, Gary and the Monster Muck Spreader will deal with the others," Nan said, turning on her engine and firing her anti-vampire juice across the field at the approaching sheep. "Woo hoo!"

By now, some of the vampire sheep had already pushed open our garden gate and were piling in! I aimed my hosepipe at them.

"Take this, you filthy flock!" I said, drenching the beasts.

WHOOSSSSSHHHHHH.

Fred climbed back up on to the shed and

threw monster missiles at as many vampire sheep as he could, while Lily rolled some at a couple of smaller lampires who were hiding in the bushes. Even Mr Tibble had stopped talking about tea and was chucking missiles at the fearsome fiends!

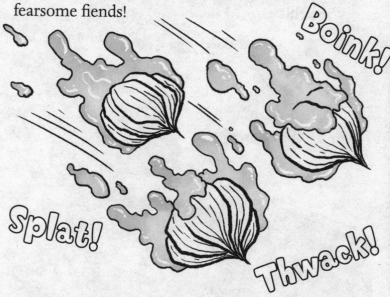

Then my mum came out with two plates of biscuits – and dropped them all over the floor!

"I thought I'd told you nasty sheep to get out of my garden!" she said, and then she picked up some monster missiles too!

Meanwhile, Nan and Gary were standing up on the Monster Muck Spreader as it trundled noisily along the grass. Nan was aiming mighty blasts of anti-vampire juice across the field and Gary fired missile after missile from the back of the vehicle.

After what felt like FIVE MILLION years but was probably only five minutes, the vampire sheep stopped their angry ~~BAA~~-ING and went very, very quiet. Then, slowly but surely, their sharp fangs disappeared, their red eyes faded back to brown, and every last one of those HORRIBLE creatures turned back into normal boring sheep.

Everybody cheered. I turned off the garden tap and sat down on the grass, exhausted! Lily cuddled one of the now-normal and very cute lambs, and Fred slid down off the shed and hugged Mr Tibble.

"Right!" said my mum, picking up the broken biscuit plate and heading for the back door. "I suppose I'd better get some more biscuits!"

"And now we really do need a nice cup of tea, my dears," said Mr Tibble, wiping his garlicky hands on his trousers before going back into his house.

"I'm getting too old for this!" sighed Nan

Helsing, as she and Gary drove over to our garden gate on the muck spreader.

They climbed down and joined us in the garden, which was *littered* with soggy baguettes and garlic bulbs.

"It was in the grass, see," said Nan.

"What was?" I asked.

"The bad magic!" said Nan, doing a little salute and offering us a garlicky hand to shake. "Nan Helsing at your service. Semi-retired beast hunter. And Gary here be the guardian of the gateway to Beastopia!"

"Beasto-what-now?" I asked.

And that was when I finally found out the BIG secret of **Knobbly Bottom**, which means that YOU will too, because Nan told us EVERYTHING.

The reason why **Knobbly Bottom** is so WEIRD is because it is built on top of what was once an underground monster city called **Beastopia**. In the olden days it was like a normal city except underground and made out of evil!

The good news is that the Helsings, aka the beast hunters, defeated all the nasty creatures, sealed the gateway AND put a massive freezer over it.

BUT, as you may have guessed, there is also some NOT so good news. A bit of leftover BAD MAGIC is still floating around down there, and the thing about leftover BAD MAGIC is this: it doesn't like being locked underground with a big freezer on top of it. So every now and again, it finds its way up to **Knobbly Bottom**. Nan said that this time it had seeped into the grass in the field behind our house, so when the poor sheep ate it – they turned into vampires! That's what we saw happening out there when the normal sheep CHANGED after munching away!

Then she told us we can't tell *anyone* about **Beastopia** because it is TOP SECRET. If the government found out, they would close off **Knobbly Bottom** and make everyone move from their homes. OR, worse than that, the bad magic might fall into the WRONG HANDS.

"But don't worry, duckalucks, I have neutralized the poisoned field and the new grass will grow back right as rain!" said Nan Helsing. "And Gary here has resealed the gateway and stuck a *second* big freezer over it."

The she hopped back up on to her muck spreader and revved up the engine. "Right, I am off on my holibobs. You did good here today, though, kiddilumps! You are officially Knobbly Bottom beast hunters now. Keep your eyes open for anything strange while I's away!"

"But, but – what if we need your help?" I shouted up to her.

"You'll be fine. Besides, Gary here will have anything you needs," she said, revving up her engine.

"But-but he's a child-eater?" I said.

"Oh, don't worry about that," said Gary. "That sign's just to keep kids away from my shop. The gateway's right underneath it, see. Don't wants them waking the bad magic with their nagging and noising. I'm actually a vegan, you know. I don't really eat children."

"Not unless they're covered in ketchup hey, Gary!" said Nan. "Jokes! Your faces! Welcome to the village, duckalucks!"

And with that, Nan rode off across the field, leaving Fred, me and Lily staring after her with our mouths wide open.

Then my mum finally came back out with a plate FULL of biscuits. Mr Tibble arrived too with a huge pot of tea, and we toasted the brave heroes (us).

Now I would love to tell you that this story

ends here, with us all smiling and happy and living happily ever after just like in a fairy tale.

But that would be a **LIE**. Because this is NOT a fairy tale. It is a true story and true stories do not always end the way you want them to. Especially ones about vampire sheep.

But if you're the kind of person that would rather have a fairy-tale ending than the TRUTH, then STOP reading after the next line.

**THE END. DEFINITELY THE END.
NOTHING MORE TO SEE HERE.**

But if you ARE brave enough to know that TRUE stories about bloodsucking beasts might end in a more terrifying way, then have a look at the REAL ending.

CHAPTER TWENTY-TWO

The real true ending

Later that day, Mr Tibble and Gary the Not So Great and Evil Child-Eater went home, and my mum went inside to make us some dinner (NOT pizza or garlic bread!).

Me and Fred were in the garden tucking into some celebratory emergency jelly babies, and Lily was playing with a couple of cute lambs that looked very happy not to be vampires any more.

That was when I realized something really, really bad. Even worse than the time I ate a piece of chocolate cake I had dropped on the floor only to realize it was not chocolate cake at all but MUD (or worse).

We had been so caught up in our epic, vampire sheep battle action, we had forgotten something.

A VERY big something.

A very big, woolly something called…

"**BAA**FACE!" shouted Fred in alarm, pointing at the huge figure that had just strolled into our garden.

BAAface, the super-NASTY vampire sheep leader, was standing on his hind legs looking even BIGGER and ANGRIER than ever. He took a step toward us.

"BAA-Da-Bing, BAA-Da-Boom, kiddos!" He growled and bared his teeth at Lily and her lambs.

"UH-OH!" I yelped, dropping my jelly babies.

"Stay away from her, BAAface," warned Fred, picking up his pan.

"What're you gonna do, boy?" BAAface laughed, taking a step closer to Lily and the lambs. "Make me a pancake?"

Summoning my big-sister bravery powers, I ran over and stood in front of Lily.

"Leave my sister alone!" I shouted. "I am warning you. I have superpowers!"

"Thanks to you lot, I'm gonna need a new army," said BAAface. "Maybe I'll turn a few of you humans into vampires this time…"

"No you jolly well won't!" I said, running

over to the hosepipe and aiming it at BAAface.

"Goodbye, BAAface!" I shouted and tried to turn the outdoor tap on – but it was stuck! I tried again but it was no good! The tap was totally jammed!

"Oh no," said BAAface, smiling, his fangs dripping with drool. "Did you mean you had stupid-powers?"

Just then, Fred raced over with his big pan and whacked the jammed garden tap as hard as he could. Finally water came gushing out of the hosepipe and all over that beastly BAAface.

"Third rule of army training!" said Fred as BAAface fizzled with the smelly steam and became a normal sheep right before our eyes. "Never go anywhere without a big pan."

"Why the heckedy-doo-dah would soldiers in the army need a big pan, or a wooden spoon for that matter?" I said as BAAface strolled off into the field, his sunglasses falling to the ground and breaking in half.

"They wouldn't. But an army chef would!" he said proudly. "And my dad is one of the best there is!"

Then my mum came out to tell us that dinner was ready, which was lucky really because BATTLING BEASTS was hungry work.

So there you have it. The real true ending. I hope it wasn't too scary for you. If it makes you feel any better, I promise that this time we really HAD defeated ALL of the vampire sheep, and they did NOT come back.

And you will not believe what my mum said over dinner. She finally uttered the words I'd been DYING to hear ever since we moved to **Knobbly Bottom**...

"Maybe we should move back to Leicester."

I opened my mouth to say a big fat "YES, PLEASE" – but that was when I realized I didn't *want* to leave **Knobbly Bottom** any more.

It might not have a soft play centre or a big Tesco or lifts with pressy buttons, BUT it had magic and Nan Helsing and Fred!

Also, if any more beasts appeared with sharp teeth and evil plans, we might have to save the world again.

After all, I was a beast hunter now.

THE END

But keep going for some extra material!

NAME: BAAFACE

SCARE FACTOR:	10
BRAVERY:	6
FIGHTING SKILLS:	7
NAUGHTY SCALE:	10

LIKES: Being evil and shouting "Baa-Da-Bing"

DISLIKES: Garlic

SUPERPOWER: Turning sheep into vampires

FUN FACT: He loves watching EweTube.

NAME: MAGGIE MCKAY

CHARACTER FILE		
SCARE FACTOR:		4
BRAVERY:		10
FIGHTING SKILLS:		9
NAUGHTY SCALE:		8
LIKES: Biscuits		
DISLIKES: Not being allowed biscuits		
SUPERPOWER: Big-Sister Bravery Powers		
FUN FACT: She is super brilliant at hide-and-seek.		

NAME: LILY MCKAY

SCARE FACTOR:	1
BRAVERY:	9
FIGHTING SKILLS:	5
NAUGHTY SCALE:	6

LIKES: Baby animals

DISLIKES: Spiders and scary sheep

SUPERPOWER: Cuteness

FUN FACT: She wants to be a superhero when she grows up.

NAME: MUM (AKA LUCY MCKAY)

SCARE FACTOR:	6
BRAVERY:	10
FIGHTING SKILLS:	8
NAUGHTY SCALE:	5

LIKES: Chocolate

DISLIKES: Wasps and flat-pack furniture

SUPERPOWER: Mum Bravery Powers

FUN FACT: She has a secret stash of chocolate hidden in the … now that would be telling!

NAME: NAN HELSING

SCARE FACTOR:	2
BRAVERY:	10
FIGHTING SKILLS:	10
NAUGHTY SCALE:	7

LIKES: Defeating beasts

DISLIKES: Beasts and bad magic

SUPERPOWER: Ninja, knitting and beast hunting

FUN FACT: She was in a band called the
Hairy Rhubarb.

CHARACTER FILE

NAME: FRED TIBBLE

SCARE FACTOR:	1
BRAVERY:	8
FIGHTING SKILLS:	7
NAUGHTY SCALE:	3

LIKES: Cooking

DISLIKES: Being hungry

SUPERPOWER: Can do ANYTHING with a spatula

FUN FACT: He owns twenty-four wooden spoons.

NAME: MR TIBBLE
(AKA FRED'S GRANDDAD)

SCARE FACTOR:	0
BRAVERY:	9
FIGHTING SKILLS:	2
NAUGHTY SCALE:	1

LIKES: Tea

DISLIKES: Running out of tea

SUPERPOWER: Making tea

FUN FACT: He is an ex-world-welly-wanging champion.

NAME: GARY THE GREAT AND EVIL CHILD-EATER

SCARE FACTOR:	7
BRAVERY:	8
FIGHTING SKILLS:	7
NAUGHTY SCALE:	6
LIKES: Peace and quiet	
DISLIKES: Noisy children	
SUPERPOWER: Guarding the gateway to Beastopia	
FUN FACT: He is actually a vegan.	

Anti-Vampire-Sheep Garlic Bread

Ingredients

60g butter, softened

2 garlic cloves (or more if your vampire sheep problem
is severe)

1 tsp dried parsley

1 part-baked white baguette

Note: Remember to ask a grown-up to help you when
you're using sharp knives and a hot oven.

Method

1. Heat the oven to 200°C/180°C fan/gas mark 6.

2. To make the garlic butter, peel and crush the garlic cloves and mix them thoroughly into the softened butter with the parsley.

3. Slice the baguette into about 12 pieces, but not all the way through. Leave the base intact to hold it all together.

4. Spread a hefty amount of garlic butter in between each slice of bread.

5. Wrap the baguette in foil, place on a tray and bake for 5 mins.

6. Unwrap the foil from the top of the bread and cook for another 4 mins so it can get nice and crispy.

7. Serve warm or use to defend yourself, your family and your town from pesky vampire sheep.

Knobbly Bottom
Beasts And How To
Banish Them

The Helsings' guide to banishing all
manner of evil and terrifying beasts

VAMPIRE SHEEP
(the younger ones are known as lampires)

WHAT THE HECKERS ARE THEY

They have glowing red eyes, fangs as sharp as
knives and they can grow up to twice the size
of a normal sheep.
This bloodthirsty
group of gangsters are
led by Baaface – the
biggest and baddest of
them all. They will do
everything he says and
follow him around
like, well, sheep.

ABILITIES
Unlike your average everyday human vampire, these sneaksters are able to go out in the sunlight because their thick woolly coats protect them from its rays. They are clever, cunning and can turn normal sheep into vampires by nipping the poor grass-gobblers on the neck.

LIFE GOALS
To create an evil army of vampire sheep and take over the world. Once in charge, they plan to move into our homes and make humans live in fields for a change!

LIKES
Being evil, rump steaks and blood.

DISLIKES
Every single human in the world. Even your gran and she's lovely.

WEAKNESSES
Garlic, holy water and counting themselves.

HOW TO BANISH THEM
A heavy dose of anti-vampire juice (garlic and holy water) will do the trick, me ducks.

ACKNOWLEDGEMENTS

As this book is part of my ongoing mission to make my children laugh, I must thank my daughters – Isla and Cleo. They are every bit as brave and hilarious as Maggie and would have no problem defeating an army of vampire sheep.

I would also like to say a MASSIVE thank you to my fantastic agent – Anne Clark – for giving me invaluable advice and believing in my writing (and for stopping me from going full Buffy the Vampire Slayer)! I wouldn't be a children's author without her.

Thank you to my brilliant editor Julia Sanderson for her guidance and support and for loving Maggie, Mum and Lily as much as I do, and to Harriet, Sarah, Hannah and the rest of the Scholastic team for championing Knobbly Bottom and being the nicest people ever. I must also say a HUGE thanks to illustrator Jeff

Crowther for bringing my characters to life so perfectly!

Thanks to my parents Madeline and Jim, for not only encouraging me to follow my dreams, but for "forcing me" to move to the countryside when I was a child and unwittingly providing me with the seed of an idea for a story.

I must also thank Sam Attenborough for helping me to trust the universe and follow my heart, Alex Milway and Katie Lee for the invaluable advice on my first draft and Michael Cameron and Emmaline King for the comedy inspiration, Pomodoro and of course, Ketchup!

I am also very grateful for my amazing writing crew, Kirsty, Katie, Lucy, Kat and Lorna – for the endless support and kicks up the bum. I would have given up years ago without their encouragement.

PLUS, a special thanks to all the inspirational women in my life, Laura Clark, Madeline Clark, Tamsin Winter and Emma Howard – for always having my back.

And finally, thanks to the countryside for providing me with loads of weird and wonderful ideas!

Look out for the next book in the series...

THE
BEASTS of
KNOBBLY
BOTTOM

RISE
OF THE
ZOMBIE
PIGS

EMILY-JANE CLARK

18/8/23

PILLGWENLLY